AFTERMATH

MARILYNN LAREW

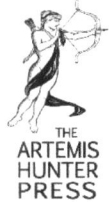

THE
ARTEMIS
HUNTER
PRESS

Artemis Hunter Press
20 New Park Road
New Park, Pennsylvania 17352

Publisher's Note: This is a work of fiction. Names, characters, places, and incidents are a product of the author's imagination. Locales and public names are sometimes used for atmospheric purposes. Any resemblance to actual people, living or dead, or to businesses, companies, events, institutions, or locales is completely coincidental.

AFTERMATH Marilynn Larew -- 1st ed.
ISBN-13: 978-0-9910912-7-0

for Karl

CHAPTER 1

Baltimore, Maryland
February 1980

"Mother! Jack wants to get married!" Elizabeth's message on the answering machine sounded increasingly anguished after the tenth repeat. Didn't she know I was out of town? Did I want to deal with that when I was dead on my feet, after the drive down from Philadelphia? I did not. Wasn't it enough that I had spent the last twelve hours being very polite to a suspicious Philadelphia cop? Being polite to a foreign cop is bad enough to cause permanent colic; I do not have to practice marriage counseling at midnight as well. I fast-forwarded over Elizabeth and heard Jack's voice.

"Pay no attention to her, Annie. We'll work it out. You may hear from a buddy of mine from Viet Nam named . . ."

1

The doorbell shrilled over Jack's exasperated voice.

". . . Charlie Magee. He thinks somebody's . . ."

The doorbell shrilled again insistently.

". . . trying to kill him. I told him you'd give him a price." He laughed. "Didn't say what kind."

There were more messages on the machine. I'd been out of town for a week, and the number of people who wanted to sell me something or consult me about something was exceeded only by the number of frantic calls from my daughter begging me to call back and defend her from the awful fate of having to marry a man she loved and had been living with for two years. What's a mother to do? Try ignoring the doorbell, for one thing. Maybe if I turned off the light and crept up the stairs whoever it was would go away. I turned off the light, and the bell shrilled again. I was halfway up the steps when I heard a car backfire. Whoever it was quit ringing the bell and began to pound on the door. I shrugged. Whatever made me think that I could just come home and go to bed like a normal person? I slipped the 9 mm automatic out of its holster and went back down the steps of my Charles Village row house cautiously. I looked at the silhouette outlined in sodium vapor light on the glass in the top half of the door. It appeared to be a man, tall and slender. The man heard the car return before I did and flattened himself against the area wall. A neat hole appeared in the glass just where his shoulders had been and not a whole hell of a distance from where my head currently was. I leveled the gun and opened the door a crack, and he slipped quickly through it. He seemed to be breathing just a mite heavily as he stood there looking at me and the gun.

"Jack sent me," he said.

"It sounds like I'm running a speakeasy," I muttered, looking at the glass that would have to be replaced in the morning. This morning, I thought wearily. If it's not one damned thing, it's another. I motioned him into my office, which is where the living room used to be when my row house was just a house. It serves as a sitting room as well. I pulled the curtains, and turned on a light. We looked at one another. What he saw was a middle-aged woman with graying hair, blue-green eyes, and a slightly thickening waist from too many Big Macs on the job and too much gin off it. He did not seem unduly impressed.

"Jack said you're good," he said, wrinkling his brow dubiously.

"What he probably said was that I was cheap," I replied, gesturing for him to sit down on the chair by the desk. I lit the gas fireplace logs and took the chair behind the desk. "From the hole in the glass, I'd say those were not backfires."

"Somebody's trying to kill me."

"That's nice," I replied. "Why?"

"I don't know," he answered and shrugged his shoulders.

And nice shoulders they were. They went with a lean body, snaky paratrooper hips, a mop of curly black hair just touched with gray, and mild blue eyes. He looked to be forty-five, maybe older, a bit old, actually, to be a good friend of Jack's. Jack is a mere baby of thirty-five who started his photographic career in

3

Viet Nam, but that was late in the war. The guy's nose was just a nose, but his chin was formidable, square and black with post-five o'clock shadow, which he was raking over with one long-fingered hand. His hand seemed to be shaking slightly. He frowned, held his hands out in front of him, and they stopped shaking. He evidently wasn't the sort of man who allowed his hands to shake. He looked to be black Irish, and he was sending me a signal that said "I'm male" so strongly that the waves were almost visible. Despite the hour and my fatigue, I felt myself sending the return signal, and that made me mad. I like to do my own sending, consciously, not involuntarily. I hauled in the "I'm a girl, isn't it nice that you're a boy" flags.

"Why do you think someone is trying to kill you?"

"I don't know."

"What are you into?" I asked roughly. "Drugs, a gambling debt, somebody's wife?" With a long week behind me, I was not too suave, and I didn't like my reaction to him. If I got nasty enough, maybe he would take offense and leave, and I could go to bed. What patience I had was used up with the Philadelphia police by about noon. Of course, if I hadn't managed to find unsuspected depths of patience in my tarnished soul, I would be sleeping quietly in the Philadelphia jailhouse now. It's funny how that helps one dredge up patience.

He shook his head no. "No drugs, no gambling, and nobody's wife, not even my own. The last one left two years, six months, four days, and"—he looked at his watch—"seven hours ago."

Interesting that he knew the time precisely. "Why would anybody want to kill you?"

"Lady," he said shortly, "if I knew that I wouldn't need you."

"Jack sent you? Jack who?"

He eyed me speculatively. "Jack Winslow, the all-American photographer. Just back from Zimbabwe or Bali or somewhere. We always thought he worked for the Agency."

"Who's we?"

"Oh, just some people I knew once."

"Look, friend," I exploded, "fencing is beyond me at this hour. Do you have a name to go with the bullet hole?"

"Charlie Magee."

"Okay, Charlie . . ."

"Don't call me Charlie."

"Okay, Mr. Magee . . ."

"Oh, shit," he said crossly. "Call me Magee."

I could see that my girlish charm was working in its usual fashion. Perhaps it was the hour. Perhaps it was the rather large check nestling in my purse from Philadelphia Heritage, Inc., for finding the gang that had been cleaning out historic houses in the Philadelphia area. I had planned to use that money to go somewhere warm, somewhere where the soft trade winds blew. Somewhere where I could sip rum punch, lie on the sand, and find a broken-down charter boat captain who was into poor middle-aged women rather than rich old ladies or muscular young persons of the same gender. Anything to escape the weather in Baltimore in February, to get over the post-Christmas hangover and get ready for another birthday. Which would be a good deal nicer than investigating the source of incoming rounds. If that was what he wanted. Let's face it, most of it was resistance to his masculinity. Why would I do that? Normally, I wouldn't. The fact that there are boys and girls is one of the few agreeable arrangements in a life that is otherwise nasty, brutish, and short, but Charlie Magee looked like trouble, pressed down and overflowing.

"Have you been to the police?"

"Yeah. They think I'm wacko."

"Are you?"

"What?"

"Wacko."

He rubbed his jaw again. "I wouldn't have said so, but who knows?"

Somehow that was comforting. In the twentieth century anybody who knows he's sane hasn't been paying attention. I looked closely at him. He might be fifteen years older than Jack, or maybe he had just had a mean life. Tiny care lines radiated out from his eyes and deeper grooves bracketed his mouth, giving him the look of a man who had sucked a lemon too long while staring into the sun. I caught myself wondering what it would be like to make those lines go away. You are, I told myself, old enough to know better. I knew those lines would not go away. They are part of the bad boy package, and it is a package I have fallen for too often in the course of a mildly misspent life. Let me help you make it through the night, I thought. Make you a pallet on the floor. Apparently, age does not bring wisdom, at least about the possibility of comforting a black Irishman with Byronic good looks. I was radiating back again. I turned down the voltage.

"Look," I said, "I may be good, but I'm not much good right now. It's been too long a day. Whatever you want will have to wait until tomorrow." I stood up. "Come back then, and we'll see."

He stood up. "You got a back door?" he asked wearily.

I suddenly realized that not only was he as tired as I was, but somebody was shooting at him, and my fine intentions dissolved. A desire to light up the life of a stranger, however, had not made me entirely foolish.

I picked up the phone and dialed the number I knew next to best. My stomach curdled when I heard Elizabeth's voice.

"Mother, where have you been? Why haven't you called?" She could certainly raise a nice tone of accusation at nearly one in the morning.

"I've been in Philadelphia for a week, Elizabeth. Is Jack there?"

"What do you mean, is Jack here?"

"What I mean is: is Jack there? I need to talk to him."

"Mother!"

"Elizabeth, I did not call you at one a.m. to discuss your marital status. I need to talk to Jack."

She slammed the receiver down on the table, and soon Jack picked it up.

"Yeah, Annie," he said, sleep clogging his voice.

"Your friend from Viet Nam. What does he look like?"

7

He grunted. "He's dark, about six-one, slender, blue eyes . . ."

"With incoming rounds."

"Really?" Mild interest replaced the sleep in his voice.

"You ought to see the hole in my door."

"Put it on his bill."

"I intend to."

I gestured to Magee, and he took the phone.

"Will you identify me, Jack?" He listened a minute and shrugged. "It's a long story, and it's been a long day. Just tell her I'm not Jack the Ripper."

I took the phone back.

"He's not Jack the Ripper."

Since he was not Jack the Ripper I took him upstairs, handed him a set of sheets and a towel from the hall linen closet, and introduced him to the spare bedroom and the hall bathroom. Fate is always so good to me. What I really needed is a man who looks like a black Irish Clint Eastwood in the spare bedroom. It's always the wrong bedroom. I closed my bedroom door on him, but the emissions came right through it.

CHAPTER 2

The smell of coffee woke me. For the moment I could not think who might be making coffee unless I had died and gone to heaven. Heaven was not actually the destination most of the people who know me have predicted, and Diva, the cool, white semi-Siamese who shares my bed by taking her half out of the middle, would not make coffee if she could. Besides, while I was in Philadelphia I had left her to the tender mercies of David, the artist who rents the basement apartment, and she wasn't speaking to me. That would end the first time she wanted to be fed; she has principles, but she never allows them to interfere with her meals.

Suddenly, I remembered to put on a shirt and a pair of jeans before I went downstairs. Jack had sent me a client. He did not have to find out what I usually wear to bed, especially if he was still transmitting two hundred-proof sex. He was either well-trained by the wife who had subsequently left him, or he was a self-made man. He had decoded the coffeemaker and found the French bread I keep in the freezer. He had also found the *Sun*, but he had left all but the sports page virgin. I poured myself a cup of coffee and tried to find something to complain about. Diva, the traitor, was curled up on his lap purring. He grunted a welcome and went on reading about the football team the city might adopt to replace the Colts, who had been kidnapped a few years back and forced to labor on the Astroturf in Indianapolis. I took the front page and settled down to pretend there wasn't a stranger at my breakfast table.

The haze gradually cleared. Nothing much had changed. Terrorists were still nasty people, and the Pentagon still preferred six hundred-dollar ashtrays. Just the usual death and taxes, which was marginally better than the Two-headed Calf and Father Marries Son after Sex Change Operation stories of the supermarket rags. He finished before I did. Ignoring my existence, he rinsed his dishes, dried them, and put them away, wiped the crumbs off the table, and left. I felt silly as I rinsed and wiped and put away my dishes and wiped my crumbs off the table. If it hadn't been for the grunt, I might have thought I had become invisible overnight.

Okay, if that's the way he wants to play it, I thought. I walked down the hall and looked at the front door. The bullet hole was still in the glass. On the floor I found a slightly misshapen hunk of lead. Well, we hadn't imagined it. Somehow I hadn't thought we had. I opened the door and did not stuff my fist in my mouth fast enough to keep a slight cry from emerging. I like to be cool, but it's not every day I find a mutilated cat on my front step.

I might have counted to two before he arrived at my side. Maybe three. We stared down at the bloody remains of a white cat, its bowels trailing loose on a body that lay crumpled, like a broken doll. With a shaking toe I nudged the poor thing. It was stiff. I turned on my heel. It wasn't Diva. It was too young, and it had a round head. Diva's head is long. Despite the fact that I had just seen her at the breakfast table, I had to see Diva to convince myself that she was still alive. When I found her in her usual daytime post under the bottom shelf in my closet, I felt some better but not much. I grabbed an old towel from the linen closet and went back downstairs to find Magee trying to move the cat's various broken extremities. I looked an enquiry.

"Been dead several hours," he said.

Goody, goody, I thought, the medical examiner hath spoken. Silently I stepped over the cat's body and looked down the steps and up and down the street. Nothing seemed out of place. There was no blood on the steps, and what was around the cat was dried to a rusty brown. I put the towel over the cat.

"I suppose you would have noticed if it had been there last night."

"You suppose right."

I bent over and tried to pick up the little corpse with the towel. Its hind-quarters were stiff, but its head lolled on a broken neck. Before I could stop myself, I retched.

"Let me do it," he offered. "I'm used to it."

"You're used to dead cats?"

"I'm used to corpses."

How much would my self-esteem suffer if I let a not-quite client clean up my front stoop? Not much, I decided, mentally erasing the charge for the broken window from his bill. I told him where the garbage can was, and he removed the cat.

I sat behind my desk and looked blindly out onto Twenty-Fifth Street while he got a bucket of water and cleaned the tile floor. One more kindness and I was either going to have to alienate him completely or give him a discount. Alienating him was easier. And cheaper. And more my style.

"You don't seem to mind bullets," he said and dropped into the client's chair.

I jumped.

"I'm sorry," he said.

"I'm relatively used to bullets," I replied. "Dead cats I can do without."

"I can do without bullets," he replied.

I gathered myself together.

"Okay, let's hear your story. Do you have the kind of playmates that leave dead cats around?"

"I don't think so."

"You said somebody was trying to kill you. How?"

"Just the good, old-fashioned way, by shooting at me and trying to drive my car off the road. The cat doesn't seem to fit. Maybe it belongs to you. Do you have the kind of playmates that leave dead cats around?"

I ran through the most recent playmates. A very nasty little druggie came to mind, as did a mildly degenerate junior high school girl. Maybe the cat was mine. I shook my head.

"Tell me what you want."

"I want you to find out who is trying to kill me and why."

"That's it?"

"That's it."

"You don't want me to do anything about whoever after I find out?"

I looked at him again. His eyes were hooded and his jaw mulish.

"No." He didn't look much like a man who asked for help in little personal problems. He didn't look much like a man who asked a woman for help either.

"How is it that you're used to corpses?" I asked.

"I used to be a paramedic."

"What are you now?"

"Nothing."

"Nothing?"

"That's right."

"Tell me."

"I think somebody tried to kill me last Monday." He paused meditatively. "Either that, or I'm having the world's longest streak of bad luck." He looked dubiously at me.

I looked dubiously back at him. He was black Irish, all right. John Wayne was a real blabbermouth in comparison. And in touch with his feelings. I felt irritated. I always feel irritated if I have to pretend there isn't somebody at my breakfast table. The fact that he was irritated to be at my breakfast table didn't help.

"Look, Charlie—"

"Don't call me Charlie."

"Look, Charlie, we can waltz around here, if you want to, while you decide whether or not you want to tell me what's going on. I don't have anything better to do than sit here and look at your body, which is quite decorative. It raises the tone of the office. It also raises the tone of the office to get a case of attempted murder. If that's what it is. I don't know how to thank you. Of course, I haven't the faintest idea what's going on, except that there's a hole in my front door." I threw the little hunk of lead at him, and he caught it automatically. "If you're right, there's going to be a hole in that lovely bod, too, and wouldn't that be a pity."

He frowned ferociously at me. I went on breathing.

"Funny things are happening," he said.

"Will you for God's sake tell me about them or stop wasting my time?"

He sighed heavily. "I don't know if any of it is connected."

"And I never will either if you don't tell me," I growled.

"I think it began last Friday night. I was on nights. We were coming back from a run to Bon Secours. It was maybe five fifteen, five twenty, and the light was almost gone. It wasn't doing anything, but it had been overcast all day, and it was almost dark. My partner was driving. We're on Hollins Street, going to turn down Warwick and hit Frederick, when we pass the intersection with Lipps Lane. For some reason, I'm looking down Lipps Lane, and I see something come out of a window. It looks like a body. I tell my partner to stop, but he doesn't hear me, because he's talking. It's his wife's night to go bowling, and he thinks she's balling instead, and he's been talking about it since four fifteen. I yell at him to stop, and he slams on the brakes. I tell him what I thought I saw, and we sit there arguing for a minute, and finally he says, 'What the hell,' and turns down Warwick and comes back up Lipps Lane, heading back toward Hollins. It comes to a point there."

"I know the intersection. I did some work for a place that makes brooms there."

"Maryland Fiber."

"Right."

"We're looking to see whether I'm crazy or not, and we see this guy down, and we stop. He's landed feet first, facedown, and is laying at right angles to the building. You know the building?"

I nodded. "Big brick loft building, five, six stories high in the back, less up toward Hollins Street. It has a machine shop in it, a paint and varnish place, and four or five other things."

"Eight stories toward Warwick. I look up. No windows open. I can't see where he came from, but from the nature of the injuries, it had to be at least a three-story fall. I did a life scan ABC survey and a head-to-toe and toe-to-head full body survey."

"ABC life scan?"

"Checking to see if his airway was clear, if he was breathing, if he had a heartbeat."

"And?"

"Yes to all three. He had facial trauma, facial fractures, lacerations to the head; he was bleeding from the nose and ear, which means a possible skull fracture, possible neck injuries, abdominal and back trauma—"

"Is all this germane?"

His eyes came back from the memory of his examination.

"Probably not. I took his vital signs. My partner got out the long backboard and a cervical collar, and I applied the collar and rolled him over onto the board, checked out his front . . ."

I shifted in my chair.

"Stick with it," he snarled. "It took about as much time to do as it does to tell. Took his vital signs again, started an IV of Ringer's Lactate, wide open through a Number 16 needle, put the MAST trousers on him and inflated them." His eyes focused on me again. "You know MAST trousers?"

"No."

"Canvas or nylon, inflatable, for fractures and other things, like blood pressure. Product of the Vietnamese war. Transferred him to the stretcher and the stretcher to the ambulance and patched into Shock Trauma for a trauma consult. They authorized a second IV, I established that, and we're ready to roll. We're going wide open to Shock Trauma, and just as we get past the loading dock of the building, a black van pulls out in front of us. My partner slams on the brakes, and this big black dude gets out of the van and pulls my partner out of the ambulance and coldco—" He stopped. "Hits him," he finished somewhat lamely.

I must remember to tell him sometime that the term coldcocked derives from the old Colt Frontier .44 and not from what he thinks it does.

"The impact throws me on my ass in the well, and I hit my head, not enough to send me out completely, just enough to scramble me. I see the doors open, and this little guy comes in with his arms swinging, pulls out both the IVs, grabs the MAST tubing and jerks it out, turns the valves, letting the MAST deflate. He sees me looking at him and gives me a clout upside the head, which throws my head up against the valve of the oxygen tanks, and I go out for a while. By the time I come to, the patient is very dead, and my ass is in a sling. In fact, that's why I'm not a paramedic anymore."

"They fired you?"

"They might as well have. They will when the investigation is over."

"Why?"

"They think I'm lying. I wasn't wearing my seat belt. Nobody does. They think I forgot to set the MAST valves. They think that when my partner slammed on the brakes, my foot got tangled in the MAST tubing and ripped it out, and that's what deflated it. And killed him, of course."

"And the IVs?"

"My foot pulled them out as I fell."

There was not any indication that he had been speaking about himself. I admire cool, but this guy was ridiculous. I could see him breathing, so I had to accept the fact that he was alive; otherwise, I would have doubted it. "And you think the attempt on your life is connected with the death of this man?"

"How should I know?"

"Why should it be? Who was the guy?"

"I don't know."

"Did you recognize the other man?"

"No. It happened too fast."

"What do you know?"

"I know I saw the guy, not very well, but I saw him. I know I didn't take out the IVs with my leg. I know my foot wasn't tangled in the MAST tube. My feet were where they always were, on the stretcher rung. That gives me a place to put my feet, and it braces the stretcher if it hasn't snapped into the locks properly. The MAST pump was tucked under the patient's feet on the stretcher, where it was supposed to be. Is that enough knowledge for you?" His cool was slipping. Maybe if I pushed a little.

"Not quite. You're talking about automatic actions. How do you know if you actually carried them out? I always put my car keys in the same pocket in my pack, except when I don't."

He actually ground his teeth.

"I did not forget to set the MAST valves! It is just not possible that I forgot."

"It's not possible to leave sponges and scalpels inside people either, but it happens. Lots of things happen."

He raised his eyes and looked squarely at me and suddenly his eyes blazed, and his face grew congested with rage. He lunged across the desk toward me, hands out, reaching for my throat. I grabbed his hair and slammed his face into the desktop and rolled my chair rapidly toward the window. My gun was upstairs in the lockbox. I am hardly ever attacked in my office until afternoon. I grabbed the desk lamp around the neck and held it like a baseball bat. He looked up at me, his nose bloody, but his eyes sane again.

"Take your problem elsewhere, Charlie," I said.

"Don't call me Charlie," he said with exaggerated softness and walked out of the office like a panther.

CHAPTER 3

He slammed the door on the way out, and I heard the broken glass fall on the floor. I cleaned it up and wedged a piece of cardboard in the hole to keep the wind out. I also cleaned the blood off of my desk and sat down to plan my trip. I didn't plan it fast enough. Half an hour after Magee left, the doorbell rang. It was Saturday; therefore, it was Elizabeth, an occurrence I had not anticipated; if I had, I would have fled.

"Mother, Jack is being unreasonable," she began while she was still in the hall.

"Hello, Mother, how are you? Hello, Elizabeth, I'm fine, thank you, how are you? I'm fine. How was your trip?"

"Mother, this is no time to be funny. This is important."

"How are you is not important? Come in and sit down, Elizabeth."

Elizabeth came in and threw herself into my armchair. She ran her fingers through her long dark hair and twisted herself into the kind of contortion that she had used for sitting in chairs as a teenager. She's twenty-five and a member of the bar, with a responsible job in the federal district attorney's office, because that is one place female lawyers can get promoted, but she seemed to regress in my company. I am not suitably serious for her taste, that I know, and my job is distasteful to her, and it is not my place to tell her (again) that my private detective business had put her through law school. She still has not gotten over her father's murder. She still has not gotten over our divorce, for that matter, and that was fifteen years ago. Actually, Elizabeth does not really approve of me, and I'm not sure that I approve of her. For one thing, she seems so stuffy, but maybe that's her youth. I can no longer remember what I was like at twenty-five. I remember that I was more sophisticated at sixteen than I ever have been since, but what was I like at twenty-five? Divorced with a kid to raise, that's what.

"Would you like a cup of coffee?" I asked, hoping to stave off the inevitable for a while longer. She was going to ask me for advice, which meant she wanted me to support her position in her argument with Jack. I had managed to stay out of it up to this point. You can't win if you give advice in affairs of the heart. Or of the groin, for that matter. I was going to have to give her my advice soon, and she was going to huff out, as usual, with our relationship, as usual, under threat of permanent rupture. I thought longingly of running away from home.

"No. Mother, why can't you concentrate?"

"Well, I would like a cup of coffee," said I, coward that I am. Elizabeth followed me to the kitchen, and we sat at the table waiting for the coffeemaker to stop hissing. We looked like an ad for mother-daughter confidences or feminine deodorant spray.

"Mother, Jack wants to get married."

"Jack has wanted to get married for almost two years. What makes this different?"

She twisted her fingers together. "This time he says he's leaving if I won't marry him. Why can't we just stay the way we are?"

"Because he wants to get married."

"But I don't."

"Why not?"

"Because. Mother, you know what marriage is. It's a patriarchal device to exploit women."

"Good God, Elizabeth, what have you been reading? Marriage is probably a patriarchal device, all right, but it was designed for the orderly devolution of property."

"Mother!"

"Well, dear, you can't blame them for wanting their property to go to their own children."

"Mother, I thought you were a feminist."

"Whatever gave you that idea? Some of my best friends are men. In fact, all of my best friends are men."

"Mother, will you be serious for a minute? What am I going to do?"

"You might start by thinking for yourself instead of parroting the idiotic, inadequate, and immature thoughts of others."

She ignored that and stuck to the point. Elizabeth always sticks to the point. "But why do we have to get married? We're so happy the way we are."

"Evidently Jack is not happy the way you are."

The coffeemaker gave a terminal hiss, and I got up to pour the coffee.

"I don't want to get married. Why can't he compromise with me?"

"Elizabeth, I don't know how you compromise on being married. It's like being pregnant. Either you are or you aren't."

"Mother, you don't understand. You're on Jack's side!"

"I'm not on anybody's side, Elizabeth. And you're right. I don't understand. Why don't you want to marry Jack? You love him. He's lovable. He loves you. What's wrong with getting married? You've been living together for two years. How could somebody saying words over you make the whole thing such a threat?"

"You don't understand," she wailed again and burst into tears.

My skin began to crawl, and I wanted to shake her. I also wanted to run as far away as possible. The doorbell rang. I ran as far as the front door. It was a tall woman, tan and perilously thin. I let her in.

"Miss Carter?" she asked in a low, well-modulated voice. "My husband is missing. I would like for you to find him."

As I was seating her in the office, the doorbell rang again. It was Jack. I put him in the living room. Full house. Not quite. I went back to the kitchen. Elizabeth had reached the sniffling stage.

"There is a client in the office, and Jack is in the living room. Do you want to go upstairs?"

She nodded and fled up the back stairs. I went back to the living room.

"There is a client in the office, and Elizabeth is upstairs crying. Will you stay here, or go into the kitchen and have a cup of coffee?" I was beginning to feel like a maître d' or a stage director.

He went to the kitchen. I went back to the office.

The office is nothing special. A gray GSA desk and color-coordinated filing cabinet. A chair for me behind the desk. A large ashtray on the desk. The Kleenex box I keep in the bottom right-hand drawer of the desk, right next to the tape recorder. Add a couple of *National Geographics* about ten years old, and it could be a dentist's office, except for the arm-chair, sofa, and coffee table gathered around a fire-place with gas logs. That made the room a sitting room as well as an office.

The prospective client was sitting in the prospective client's chair, with her long, thin, tanned legs crossed. They had been good legs ten years back when they, and she, had some meat on them. A tan in February meant she could meet my hourly rate. She was holding a long, thin, tan cigarette with long, thin, tanned fingers that looked competent to hold either a golf club, the tiller of a sailboat, or a martini glass, or maybe all of the above. She had dropped about

$25,000 worth of fur on the armchair, which left only the simple little navy wool number from the same designer that Jackie Onassis uses and the simple little gold nothing from Van Cleef and Arpels on her shoulder to shield her from the cold. She was not wearing simple little gold earrings to match, but she was wearing a wedding band and an emerald the size of a cocktail olive on the third finger of her left claw. Steel-colored hair, either gray or platinum, done in a medium pageboy, eyebrows rigidly plucked and arched, and a rosebud mouth painted Day-Glo orange complemented by matching spots of orange high on her cheekbones all gave her the look of a surprised art deco poster. Her long slender face and the network of fine lines radiating from her eyes and connecting her slightly Roman nose with the rosebud mouth contradicted the flat art deco, and superimposed upon it a "Decline and Fall of the Roman Empire" overlay to give her a look of ageless decadence, a look enhanced by smoky yellow-gray eyes. A cat-sphinx and, unless I missed my guess, a nasty one.

"My name is Vivian Rowlandson. My husband, Glenn, has been missing for a week, and the police don't seem to want to do anything about it, so I suppose I'll have to. I don't know what we pay taxes for."

"Missing Persons is understaffed. And more people seem to be taking off these days. With adults, unless there are special circumstances, they usually don't bother. It's not against the law to disappear."

"So I have to pay a detective to find my husband?"

"Only if you want to find your husband," I replied and waited. She stubbed out one cigarette and lighted another, smoking in restless puffs. I counted five butts in the ashtray. That was one for every three minutes she had been in the office. She got more restless as the silence grew. I let it grow. Finally, she twitched into speech.

"My husband is fifty-seven years old. He retired from the Army at the rank of lieutenant colonel in 1972 with twenty years' service and a medical disability, and he has been ill off and on ever since. I am seriously worried about him. He may be wandering somewhere, unable to remember who he is or where he lives."

"Does he have Alzheimer's?"

"No."

"What caused his disability?"

"Stress."

"Stress?"

"He was in Viet Nam."

A fellow could certainly get stressed there, but I don't remember hearing that they retired people for that.

"Tell me about it."

"I don't really know much about it. He doesn't like to talk about it. He is a West Point graduate, of course . . ."

Of course. No ROTC cadet for this lady.

". . . and his work was difficult and dangerous. He began to have blackouts."

"Seizures?"

She shifted in her chair. "Not to my knowledge. Just blackouts."

"Has he had any blackouts since he retired?"

"Only once, a few years back, when his mother died."

"Did he disappear then?"

She glared at me; I put on a look of infinite patience, which was what this woman was going to cost me, and waited.

"For a while."

"Did he come back of his own accord?"

"No. Yes."

"Which is it, no or yes?"

"Yes."

"How long was he gone?"

"A week."

"Where had he been?"

She didn't want to answer that one.

"Where?" I repeated.

"I don't know."

"What did he say when he got back?"

"Nothing."

"What makes you think he had a blackout?"

She didn't want to answer that one either. Finally, she lifted her hand and said, "What else could it have been?"

"What did he do when he got back?"

"Nothing."

"Nothing?"

"Nothing different."

I sighed. Where did you go? Out. What did you do? Nothing. I thought it over. Maybe she had a right to be worried, maybe not. Maybe he just needed a vacation from that glare once in a while.

She reached into the leather envelope on her lap, took out a photo and handed it across the desk to me. It was a copy of a studio portrait. He was in his dress blues. They set off his wavy white hair, his deep blue eyes, and his youthful, finely chiseled profile. He was the very model of a modern major general. So many light colonels are.

"This was taken at the time of his retirement, but he has not changed, except to put on a little weight."

I nodded. "Is he driving?"

"His station wagon is missing."

"Have you reported it missing?"

"No."

"You should. It might help find him. What have you done?"

She shrugged. "The obvious. Called hospitals, searched the neighborhood, called friends. Can you start now?"

I nodded. The colonel might not thank me for finding him. If that was the case, she didn't need to know I had found him. She took another piece of paper out of the envelope. It was a check for a thousand dollars. That is really the only acceptable thing about people who can afford to hire private detectives. Their checks are negotiable.

Her address was in Garrison. I made arrangements to go out and look around, but first I was going to have to do something about Elizabeth and her marriage-avoidance. Since it was Saturday, there were only a few things I could do to find the colonel that his wife had not already done, but I could go out and search his space to give her the idea she was getting something for her money.

Jack was sitting in the kitchen staring morosely at his empty coffee cup. I poured myself a cup and looked inquiringly at him.

"No, thanks. My mouth feels like the bottom of a bird cage now. How did you and Charlie get along? I hope you can help him. I owe him."

"You're going to have to go on owing him."

"What happened?"

"I had to use blasting powder to get anything out of him. I never did get the whole story before I threw him out."

"Threw him out?"

"Only after he tried to strangle me. That guy is a walking time bomb."

"He's been one for a long time. Probably since his second wife left."

"He's a two-time loser?"

"At least. You should sympathize with that."

"I don't have any sympathy for somebody dumb enough to get married twice."

"That's where she gets it, you know," he said quietly.

"Elizabeth hardly regards me as a role model, Jack," I said defensively.

"Yes, she does. Otherwise, she never would have battered her way through law school."

"Are you telling me that she doesn't like the law?"

"No, she likes the law. She's afraid to get married because she's afraid I'll do to her what Milton did to you."

"That's nonsense, Jack. She has never admitted that Milton did anything to me. As far as she's concerned, Milton was perfect. I'm Dracula, but her father was perfect."

"She knows her father wasn't perfect, Annie, but she can't say that out loud, especially not since he was murdered. The word marriage starts her shaking, a real panic attack. And I'm tired. Annie, I'm so tired. I'm tired of hearing how rotten men are. I'm tired of hearing how rotten society is. I'm tired of being responsible for the sins of mankind. And I do mean man. I just want to get married and lead as normal a life as I can with this damn job of mine. I just want to put my arms around her and be quiet for a while."

"Go home, Jack. I'll see what I can do."

"I can't go home, Annie. I have to go to Nicaragua."

Elizabeth was facedown on my bed, sound asleep, her face stained with tears but relaxed and soft, like a child's. How could I teach her to trust when I didn't trust anybody or anything? Two years with Jack hadn't taught her to trust him, and as far as I could tell, he seemed entirely trustworthy. Who is entirely trustworthy in personal matters? If anybody is, Jack is. That's what our friends thought about Milton. You can't judge anything from the outside, that I knew, from my own marriage as well as from my work. The kid who shoots the president is always such a nice boy, from such a nice family. But turn over the nice family and watch what slimy things crawl out from under.

In the end, I chickened out again. I left her a note telling her to wait for me to get back and left. Dealing with that problem was going to turn over my log, and I didn't want to know what was underneath.

CHAPTER 4

The nice thing about the Jones Falls Expressway is that, like the Pennsylvania Turnpike, it is so badly designed that you don't dare do anything but drive, if you want to stay alive. Major renovations are supposed to solve that problem, but until they are completed, they only make it worse, and I concentrated on driving. Garrison is a funny section, a ring of farmland just west of the beltway on Reisterstown Road that is owned by old, old money, and the old, old money has so far refused to sell out and let the developers have their way with it. The result is a green belt sandwiched in between two swatches of development that are a cross between Route 1 and suburban Connecticut.

The gatepost at the foot of the Rowlandson's drive said "The Gables." I turned in and drove up the winding lane between rows of gnarled oaks standing nude and skeletal against the thin winter sky.

White-fenced pastures streaked with pockets of snow where the sun didn't hit rose with me and reminded me of the Bucks County estates I had just come from. Those had been cleaned out of treasures. This one had misplaced its master. On the military crest of the hill girdled by a circular drive stood The Gables, a many-sided Victorian house painted in proper historic preservation colors, all earth tones and high seriousness. Even the gingerbread was serious. It was as if a daughter of Charles Addams had married a son of John Ruskin. On both sides of the drive lay formal ranks of sleeping rose gardens bisected by a wide grass strip on which teak garden benches faced each other from either end. All the symmetry the house lacked the gardens provided, offset by clumps of old trees seemingly cast at the lawn in a fit of absentmindedness. Slightly dirty unmelted snow lay about their roots. Behind the house was a large stable yard with genuine stables on three sides, and the genuine stables seemed to have genuine horses in them. Even the pastures you couldn't see from the road or the drive were enclosed in white-painted rail fence. It looked like a *New Yorker* ad for single malt whiskey.

Past the stable yard, I spotted a classic MG with the top up and a leather suitcase strapped to its luggage rack. Was somebody going somewhere? The car was red like the one I had once fallen in love with. If I could just have that car, I thought, I would floss after every meal and always wear a petticoat, whether anybody could see through my skirt or not.

I thought about parking in the stable yard and going in the back just like a real person but decided against it and continued around the house to leave my ten-year-old Toyota in front. I would go in the front door, not the servants' entrance. I was going to have to convince Madame that I was not a servant if I was going to survive working for her. Why did I have to work for her? I had enough in the bank to go and play in the sun for a while. That was always a nice spine stiffener. But I took the case. Probably my insatiable curiosity.

I twisted the bell in the middle of the door and admired the gingerbread that laced the wide porch. The door opened, and I faced a slender dark man in a white jacket and dark trousers. A houseman, by God. It must be old money or a lot of it. Help is hard to find these days, good or bad.

"Good afternoon," he said in a soft, musical voice. I looked at him again. Black, but not American black. Haitian? He was about as tall as I, well-muscled, with very tidy hands and feet. His round unlined face gave away nothing. He smiled gently at my confusion. He probably smiled at everybody's confusion.

"Anne Carter. Mrs. Rowlandson is expecting me."

"Ah, yes. Come in, won't you?"

Correct historical detail ended when I crossed the threshold into a hall that had been in the hands of Andy Warhol. If only it had been as simple as a can of Campbell's tomato soup. The long hall led past two sets of closed doors on each side to a ravaged central staircase and gallery. Instead of the usual newel post and banister, somebody had put square silver-colored metal posts connected with matching chains up along black steps without risers. On top of the first posts were what I supposed were newels—twisted very bright orange things like Christmas trees, their branches twisting up and out, their sharp metal branches decorated with black baubles. Down the hall, massive carved mantels faced each other between the two sets of doors. In each fireplace was a famille verte vase of museum quality in which floated bouquets of multicolored balloons. Here and there on the black-and-white marble floor tiles were scattered small woven pieces with hallucinatory renditions of Asian and African fertility symbols, themes that were repeated on the stenciled walls. The colonel's departure was no longer a mystery; he was clearly an art critic. What was surprising was that he hadn't shot his wife on his way out.

The houseman led me to the second pair of doors on the right, the place where a rational Victorian family had a morning room, smiled again, and pushed the doors open with a little flourish. I gritted my teeth and walked in, to a room still warm with winter sun, full of soft chintz colors and poufy, comfortable furniture; a pair of love seats faced each other by the fireplace. Between them a round oak pedestal table with claw feet did duty as a coffee table, and cushions and armchairs and cozy lamps clustered around a soft rose silk Isfahan rug worth every penny of a shah's ransom. I felt like having a blackout myself.

Madame was sitting curled up on one of the love seats toasting herself before the fire. She wore blue jeans and an orange running top that matched her clown rouge but clashed madly with the decor. She was smoking one of her long brown cigarettes with nervous gestures again as she looked me over in amusement.

"Isn't the hall divine?" she asked in a high, false voice. "Such a darling little man, the decorator, and so talented."

"Is he currently at liberty, or did they lock him back up?" I asked as I sat down on the facing love seat.

She stretched and laughed. "I've always liked a little shock. Starts the juices flowing."

"Maybe," I conceded, "but can the house take it?"

She made hostess noises, and the houseman poured me a cup of coffee from the pot of a set on the oak table, a Steiff rose repoussé pattern, circa 1880, whose twin was in the Maryland Historical Society Museum. Money both old and plentiful. Mrs. Rowlandson grinned maliciously this time.

"Your husband," I said after a time spent with the coffee, which tasted like Mocha Java. Of course. Nothing Maxwell House about this house.

"Yes. Glenn. What can I tell you?"

"About him. What he did in the Army. What he's like. Why you think this requires the services of a private detective."

She put out her cigarette and immediately lit another. "Glenn's always been a bit—boyish. Army men are, you know. Duty, honor, country."

"The long gray line. The corps and the corps and the corps. I heard the speech too."

She shifted somewhat guiltily. "He's from an army family. He was born in Shanghai, but his mother was a Hopkins; they used to own half of Anne Arundel

County. He and his mother spent the war years at the family place down on the Severn. He boarded at McDonough for high school, bound for the academy from the day he was born. I met him at a dance. Garrison Forest used to have tea dances and invite the McDonough cadets. White gloves and pearls, that sort of thing."

Army family, military school, military academy. Perhaps she was right. The corps and the corps and the corps could lead to arrested development.

"I met him again at a party in Philadelphia after the Army-Navy game in, oh, 1951, I guess. I was at Bryn Mawr and he was a senior, oops, first-year man, so it was the winter of 1951. Navy won. It mattered to him. He graduated and was commissioned in 1952 and went straight to Korea. Second lieutenants of infantry were an endangered species in those days." She looked pensively at the ash on her cigarette. "I guess they always have been."

"The sergeants in the old frontier army used to say that second lieutenants would make fine officers, if they lived."

She nodded. "When he got back, they sent him to Second Army Headquarters at Fort Meade. We were married in October 1953. The bridesmaids wore autumn colors. He got bored fairly soon. I guess it was the first time he had to cope with the real army, and he never suffered fools particularly well. He applied for paratroop school, and we went to Fort Benning. He loved it. I can't tell you how he loved it. Jumping out of airplanes was never my idea of fun. I used to jump horses when I was younger, but out of airplanes?

Anyway, while he was there, he met a friend who had just joined the Special Forces. It was new in those days, quite secret, and a little raffish." She smiled. "It's still raffish, in a way." She shook her head. "In any case, he joined and fought the fabled battle of the Green Berets," she said ironically, as if it were part of the boyishness. "Silly hat. Then Fort Bragg and Hawaii. I went with him. He left me in Honolulu while he went to Thailand to train Rangers. He was so happy to be going back to the East. He could just remember China. He spoke Chinese before he spoke English."

"Good with languages?"

"Like breathing. Chinese, several Thai dialects, Laotian, Vietnamese, German, French, you name it, he speaks it. In 1957, they established a Special Forces Group on Okinawa, and I joined him there. A nice place, with a reasonable climate and decent quarters. So many Americans were there that you didn't have to know you were abroad unless you wanted to."

"He continued in Special Forces?"

"Yes. It didn't seem to hurt his career, not at first anyway. He was a captain by that time, right on schedule. People told him he ought to get out, back to paratroops, at least, but he was enjoying himself and didn't want to bother about career management."

You're not supposed to have fun, I thought, you're supposed to get your ticket punched.

"We came back to the states to Fort Bragg, but he didn't pull a whole tour before he was shipped to Laos, that was in 1959, to train people in guerrilla warfare. He was there until October 1962."

"And you?"

"Oh, I stayed at Bragg. Well, I came home for a while, and I traveled a bit, but I never got along with my father very well." She gave a bitter little smile. "I don't get on with women well either, certainly not the pious kind. So the place at Bragg was handy."

"Children?"

She grimaced. "Three miscarriages in four years, and a long dry spell while he was in Laos. No, no children."

Was she happy or sad? I couldn't tell. There was no emotion on her clown face, unless the rouge stood out a little more clearly. The end of the line for the Rowlandsons?

"Is he an only child?"

"Yes, as am I. Sad degeneration of old landed families. The end of the line." She brushed angrily at some nonexistent ash on her jersey and rapidly drank some coffee that must have been quite cold by that time. She returned to repeating her husband's 201 file in a dull voice. "After the boys were thrown out of Laos in 1962, he got career-minded. A stateside tour in the Pentagon. He hated staff slots, but it was what you were supposed to do. My father was ill at the time, and I spent my time here. I'm not much of a nurse, but sometimes one has to do what is done. He had quarters at Fort Myer and came up on the weekends. Daddy always liked him," she said irrelevantly.

"Surely the early sixties were flush times for Special Forces? Why did he get out then?"

"The old Special Forces people weren't too keen at the rapid expansion. They had to take in too many of the wrong sort. And he had a perverse streak.

When things were going well, he often did the wrong thing. Anyway, after Kennedy was assassinated, before his tour was up, he went back into Special Forces."

Just in time for the program to be assassinated too, I remembered, by brass hats who had always hated the Green Berets. With Kennedy gone, they didn't have to give lip service to counterinsurgency and could resume their pursuit of expensive weapons systems.

"This time he went to Viet Nam. He never left Special Forces after that. He hardly ever left Viet Nam, for that matter. We never did get to Germany. Probably it was just as well. I don't think I'm suited to long stretches in a provincial town in Bavaria. One can't ski all the time. When he made major he was falling behind, but he wouldn't leave Special Forces, and he hated headquarters, couldn't stay out of the field. The stress and the climate got to him, but good ones become irreplaceable, and he was a good one. He was wounded when the Montagnard camp near Khe Sanh was overrun during the siege, but they couldn't or wouldn't evacuate him for a while. Something went wrong. He never told me, but when the siege was finally lifted, they got him out and put him in the hospital. He was there for a long time, with endless lists of parasites and fever and who knows what all."

"The wound?"

"I don't think it was the wound. It was the other, and the time he had spent in those god-awful holes eating rats and hiding from the siege. It was his right leg. I think it healed all right. He feels the damp in it now and limps a little. It was the other. Anyway, after he got out of Walter Reed, we went back to Bragg, and soon he went back to Viet Nam, not as part of an A team that time." She stopped. "Do you know how they're set up?"

"Special Forces? No."

"I'll give you a book. The field units are supposed to be twelve men, one or two officers and the rest senior non-coms. Those are A teams. The rest of the lot are in B, C, or D teams, all at headquarters, support, logistics, planning, that sort of thing. He was on the B team at I Corps."

I nodded.

"Headquarters in Saigon kept meddling with the program. He kept sneaking out to the Laotian border to play. He made lieutenant colonel, but his career was shot, and all of his illnesses came back, all worse. In '72, he spent a while in Saigon in the hospital and later in Japan in another hospital, and after that they boarded him." She looked at me. "Refused to promote him and retired him at twenty years with a medical disability."

"He was still a young man. What next?"

"A contract with the CIA. He traveled some, but he couldn't go back into the mountains for long without getting sick. After everything fell in '75, he did a lot of refugee interrogation, spent a lot of time traveling to the camps, some more time in the hospital. For a while he was in business with some friends, but he wasn't any great shakes as a businessman. He got out."

"What kind of business?"

"Security."

Oh. I raised my eyebrows. "Selling arms to the Iranians?"

"No, not with Secord. Like that, though. He knew Secord from Laos. Security, arms, that sort of thing. He got mixed up in some dimwitted plan to rescue POWs and got arrested in Thailand."

"When?"

"I don't know. '78? Something like that. I can look it up. He was sick again. Instead of trying him, they sent him back, and he went into Walter Reed again. Perhaps if he could just get the parasites out of his system, he could get Southeast Asia out of his system. I don't know; maybe it's terminal."

"What does he do now?"

"Nothing much. Keeps up, a little."

Boyish? I looked around the cheerful room. Obsessed maybe, but boyish? I remembered his picture and read the tan now as jaundice, but there were still precious few lines on that young old face, not nearly enough for the kind of life he had led.

"And the blackouts? When did they start? In Viet Nam?"

"After. When he worked for the Agency."

"Does he drink?"

"Does a fish swim? Oh, I don't know that he drank—that he drinks—more than the rest of them. He drinks more now."

"A lot more?"

"Enough to stay sane. More since his mother died."

"Which was the first time he disappeared."

"Which was the first time I knew about him disappearing, yes. But don't think Freudian things. He wasn't that attached to her. Oh, most of them are, you know. To mother and apple pie. They'd rather eat fish sauce, but they all do homage to apple pie."

"They?"

"Army officers. The flag and womanhood, that sort of thing."

And what did he think of this brittle specimen, I wondered.

"What's he like?" I asked. "Temper? Routine?"

"What can I tell you? He is very controlled. No temper I ever saw. Fantastically, unbelievably reliable, brave, upright. He can do anything with a screwdriver and a bent nail. Drive anything, jump off anything, swim anything, shoot anything."

"I mean what was he like to live with?"

She stubbed another cigarette out. "I can't say," she replied coolly. "I haven't really lived with him all that much, have I?"

CHAPTER 5

Hmm. I stood. "May I see his room? If he has one. A desk. Calendar? His clothes? Did he take any? The car? And a list of friends."

We walked up that fantastic staircase and turned right into a two-room suite with a study over the morning room, and a bedroom next to it facing the stable yard that connected with a bath. I looked at her, and she opened the other bathroom door.

"My room," she said.

I went back to his.

"I'll leave you," she said. "Look at whatever you want. I think there may be some clothes missing, but I can't be sure. Phi will know."

"Fee? As in Fee, Fi, Fo, Fum?"

"Phi as in P-H-I. It means "spirit" in Tai. He's one of my husband's acquisitions. A black Tai."

And I'm a cummerbund, I thought. She stood there as I looked around Rowlandson's bedroom, wishing she'd go away. I was getting very little reflection of Glenn Rowlandson in his own space, almost as little as I had while his wife was reciting his personnel file. I wished he would prove his existence to me.

At least there had been no decorator here. A complicated marble mantel with a military print over it— Prussian soldiers in the wasp-waisted uniforms of the Napoleonic era, with frogs and shakos and lion skins, all neat and on parade. She moved around nervously, picking things up and putting them down, and I wished again she'd go away. If she left, maybe her husband would seep back into the room. She crossed to the corner window and twitched the heavy draperies.

"This was my father's room," she said inconsequentially. "He always liked Glenn. Father was in France during the war."

She was showing her age, I thought. We've had several wars since. I sighed and went back to looking for Glenn Rowlandson. The furniture was what the house demanded instead of that obscene hall: eighteenth- and nineteenth-century antiques. A chest with a small supply of underwear, black socks for evening, and a pair of thick gray wool socks for hiking or combat boots. A fair supply of dress shirts. No casual shirts. A sweater in khaki wool with leather on the shoulders and Her Majesty's label. Souvenir of a training spell with the SAS? Or an Eddie Bauer catalog. Old Orientals on the floor here and there.

She twitched again. "I'll be downstairs," she said and left me in peace.

The closet revealed a couple of dress suits, old but bespoke. A dinner jacket, ditto. An ancient gray homburg. Her father's? Dress and evening shoes. Bass Weejuns. A bunch of empty hangers. Altogether, not much of a wardrobe for a man of the colonel's wealth. And where were the old flannel pants? The khakis? There seemed to be no leisure wear anywhere. Maybe he was gone for good. I went into the study.

The winter sun had retreated, leaving the room cold, but at least there were traces of the man in this room. From the bedroom, I might have thought that Mrs. Rowlandson was running a bed-and-breakfast and had only imagined that she had a husband to misplace. The marble mantel matched the one in the bedroom and the fender and tools were equally well-polished. But at an angle in front, within easy distance for propping feet on the fender, stood a large wing chair in worn scarlet leather decorated with brass-headed tacks. The leather was slightly cracked, and the cushion bore the imprint of someone's posterior. The side table was carved and black and Oriental, with marching elephants and parasols and Buddhist persons. Thai? Laotian? A brass lamp pretending to be a candle. An empty pipe stand and a box of kitchen matches.

No Prussians in corsets over the mantel here, but an ancient Chinese travel scroll showing a tiny cavalcade of people on those lovely full-bottomed ponies, led by a person in plain but elegant robes, by his cap a magistrate. They were inching their way along a narrow path beside a roaring stream, dwarfed, as the people always are in Chinese art, by the towering misty mountains. A foot of the scroll was open under glass, three frames of the journey. The scrolls at either end rested on brackets. The Freer Gallery would kill for it. I myself would wound somebody seriously for it. Is that what the Indochinese mountains looked like? Probably.

The rest of the room was manly and western. A large desk of no particular style under the windows faced out over pasture into the trees. Desk things. An old manual typewriter. I sat in the chair and looked through the drawers. Drawer things. There was a checkbook with the stubs not made out in the top drawer. The file drawer had files, one marked "will." It was empty. A tax file, with receipts. Financial statements. A wad of fading copies of Army orders. I could come back for this stuff if I had to. A first-rate Kerman on the floor. Against the wall by the closet door stood the kind of bookshelves you used to find in doctors' and lawyers' offices, with glass doors that slid up over the books. Inside were some forgotten nineteenth-century novels, a biography of Disraeli and one of Cavour, Teddy Roosevelt's western history. At eye level, a whole shelf of Asian history in paper: classical French anthropological studies, a Harper Torchbook one-volume history of China, some Chinese and Vietnamese dictionaries, Harold Isaacs' book on the Chinese revolution. The same history of Indian art I'd had in college. Chinese art. Buddhism. The *Tao Te Ching*. Fall's *Street Without Joy*. A swatch of Vietnamese war memoirs. I opened the case and took out *A Rumor of War*. The flyleaf was inscribed "to Glenn from Vivian, Christmas, 1978." From the looks of it, never read. The same for *If I Die in a Combat Zone.* ("If I die in a combat zone/Box me up and ship me home.") After a while I knew that all the Asian history had been read and underlined, and all of the war memoirs had been presents from his wife and hadn't been read. Why had she given him those books? Was she mad? Or just dumb? She hadn't struck me as dumb. Why would he want somebody to tell him what the war was like? I closed the case.

The closet had some expensive toys: skis, old fishing equipment, a double-barreled shotgun, clean and well-cared for. Across the room by the door to the bedroom, a drinks cart stood between the windows, with good brandy and the usual whiskeys. A clear unlabeled bottle stood at the back, with no dust on it. I unscrewed the top and sniffed, and the unmistakable odor of corn liquor assailed my nostrils. I put the cap back on. Gin was low enough. Corn? Did they make corn liquor in the Laotian mountains? They probably made something fiery. The only people I ever met who didn't were the American Indians. There was no dust anywhere. Phi was a good housekeeper. I needed to talk with him. How much was missing from the closet? Outerwear? Luggage? The room was growing dim. It was time to go home and think, if my daughter would let me.

I stepped out into the hall and closed the door after me. Were the toys in the closet his or her father's? He didn't seem much given to toys. No radio, no TV, no sound system. No photographs either of his wife, his parents, himself, or his units. No Cadets on the Plain at West Point. No commendations or certificates showing he had learned to kill people with a staple, a piece of string, and a bus ticket. No brass trays or funny knives or carved elephants. Just that table and the scroll.

I listened. Dimly, from behind one or another set of doors, came the sound of music. Early Beatles. Followed by "Fifty Ways to Leave Your Lover."

Suddenly I felt tired. I went back to the morning room, but it was no longer bright and cheerful. It looked faded and shabby in the failing afternoon light. My client didn't look shocking anymore but shabby, too, like a sad marionette backstage in an empty theater.

"I'd like a list of your husband's friends, particularly the people he was in business with."

She pointed to a piece of paper on the coffee table. Three names written in a spiky hand. She used Greek e's. They didn't teach her that at Garrison Forest.

"I'd like to talk to your houseman," I said. "There are probably clothes missing."

She shrugged out of her lethargy and rang a bell. We waited; we had nothing to say to each other. There wasn't much trace of Glenn Rowlandson, Green Beret, in the house. Perhaps there had never been. Nothing happened and after a while she rang again. Again nothing. Muttering under her breath, she went into the back part of the house and returned shortly with a puzzled look on her face.

"He's not there. He's gone."

The suitcase strapped to the MG? I followed her through the kitchen and down the stairs to a bedroom and bath in the basement. The closet door was standing open. It was empty. Empty bureau drawers gaped. The double bed was stripped with the blanket folded at the bottom. There was not even a used razor blade in the bathroom wastebasket. Suddenly her face split as if the makeup had become too tight. She threw herself on the bedroom floor weeping hysterically.

It was quite dark when I got home. Of course, that only meant that it was six thirty, but I felt as if I had wrestled an alligator, gone over Niagara in a barrel, and finished off by going fifteen minutes in a clothes dryer. Maybe Elizabeth was right. Maybe I should retire and sit in a rocking chair wearing a shawl and knitting. I could manage those physical things with more composure than when I manage weeping women. In my day that sort of hysteria wasn't done. Of course it had always been done by everyone but me. Wearily I parked the car in the backyard and went in the house. It was dark. Elizabeth had gotten tired of waiting. Thank God! Alone at last. There are actually people who enjoy scenes. My former sister-in-law spent much of her adult life setting people against each other, taking offense, and phoning me to tell me how badly everybody was treating her. She enjoyed it heartily, and it put her in good shape to contest her father's will. I wondered idly whether they had ever settled the estate. I must remember to ask Elizabeth.

I made myself a bowl of milk toast. After she stopped thrashing away on the floor in the servants' quarters, Mrs. Rowlandson had washed her face, put on fresh makeup, and looked good for another hundred thousand miles. She had refused to report the red MG stolen, described her husband's station wagon to me (although not the number of its license plate), and sent me out of the house with a copy of *Inside the Green Berets* by Charles M. Simpson III, USA (Ret.).

"Bill Simpson is a darling," she told me.

I refused to inquire why she called him Bill when his name was Charles. I flipped to look at the pictures scattered throughout the volume. I found one of the author with two other men taken at Pleiku in 1966. More slender than the others, he did look mildly darling in his fatigues with the sleeves rolled up loosely, rather like a recently graduated French lycée student, beside his chunkier companions. Pale? Well, intellectual, anyway. And on him the beret was a silly hat. It suited Lee Parmley, the man in the far right of the picture. On him it was as aggressive as his jaw. If I had to choose somebody to have with me in a brawl, I'd choose Parmley. On the other hand, I wouldn't want to be stranded on a desert island with him.

The milk toast soothed my stomach. I'd better be careful, I thought. When I'm tired, my digestion goes first, then my temper, and, not too much later, I collapse, yowling for my teddy bear, and only a couple of days in bed will help. Sometimes the collapse can be staved off with gin, but for some strange reason my body is coming increasingly to reject that form of medication. Old age.

I lit the gas logs in the office fireplace and settled down with the Green Berets. I remembered the movie. If it bore any relation to reality, I didn't think I was going to like Colonel Rowlandson any more than I liked his lady. On the other hand, the colonel owned that scroll and valued it enough to put it in his private place, where he could look up and see it anytime he wanted to. I propped my feet up on my fender (black—who has time to polish brass?), looked lovingly at the Hiroshige print of a scene on the Inland Sea, my favorite thing and right where I could see it anytime I wanted to. I consoled myself with the thought that John Wayne movies usually bear the same resemblance to reality that Road Runner cartoons do.

I had read as far as page ninety-nine, in which the author was describing how silly the movie was, when the doorbell rang. I put the book facedown on the table by my chair and went out into the hall to peer through the glass in the door. The figure silhouetted in the dim light from the street looked familiar. Oh, well, I thought, why not? It's been a perfect day so far.

Charlie Magee followed me into the office and sank down on the sofa. The crisp dark curls were in disarray, as was his face. He rubbed his chin wearily. "I apologize. I guess." He had to force the words out. Not his usual style, I thought.

"Okay."

"You want me to start again?"

"If you'll tell me what's bothering you," I replied, "without my having to pull each word out of you with pliers."

He looked at me uncertainly.

"Jack is a friend. He says he owes you. I'm willing to listen."

His eyes strayed to the book about the Special Forces. (Never call them Green Berets, I had learned. That's the hat.)

"What's that about?" he asked.

"I was thinking of joining until I found out you had to jump out of airplanes."

"It's not that big a deal," he replied absently and rubbed his chin again.

"Being suspended is not what worries you," I said.

"No. I guess not. If they fire me I can always train Contras or join the South African Defense Force."

"If you want to find a war to play in, I hope you can find something more respectable," I commented tartly.

That black Irish grin flickered for a moment. "They pay in gold."

"Neato, let me give you the number of my Swiss bank account. Now, what is it that's bothering you?"

"Somebody's trying to kill me, I think. I can't tell. I may be imagining it."

"You didn't imagine those shots last night."

"No," he agreed hesitantly, "but . . ."

A couple of hours and three beers later, I had his story and had tucked him away in the spare bedroom again. It was a weird little story. I wasn't as convinced as he was that he hadn't forgotten to fix the valves on the MAST trousers, but he certainly seemed to have become accident-prone recently. Actuaries would become incoherent if all the things that had happened to him in the past week were coincidental. First, the dead man, a short, stocky man wearing a business suit, who must have come out of a window at least three stories up. A day later, when Magee was driving at high speed on the beltway, coming up the long hill from Wilkens Avenue, a tire blew while he was trying to overtake a large truck that wasn't supposed to be in the third lane. It was a new tire. He wrestled the car away from the concrete divider and away from the truck and finally got it slowed down, but it had been a near thing. Firestone had replaced the tire with apologies and an odd look.

Two nights after that, he was driving home on Route 40 when a truck had tried to sideswipe him on the bridge over the Patapsco River. It was at high speed again; nobody ever drives the speed limit on that stretch of road. He made sparks on the side of the bridge getting away.

The next night as he was coming out of a bar in Irvington near the firehouse where he worked (if he still had a job), he thought somebody followed him to where his car was parked and took a shot at him. He thought he recognized the sound as the bullet zipped past his head. He thought he did, but the next day he couldn't find any trace of a slug and had to stop looking after people began to stare at him.

He lived way out in the country in a small, isolated house near the Howard County fairground, and thought he had heard somebody prowling around outside the next night. When he looked the next morning, he found what might be some tracks, but they were faint, and he couldn't be sure. By that time, he was so jumpy he couldn't tell what to believe, and he remembered that Jack's girlfriend's mother was a private detective. He almost blushed when he told me that. He would have to be jumpy to look for help. He called Jack and got my number, but I was still in Philadelphia, and when nothing happened for a day or two, he thought he had been imagining it.

Last night he had come into town to take a girl to dinner and a movie, and somebody followed them out of the parking lot, not trying to hide it any, but the woman couldn't see anything, and, as he said, you can't tell much at night anyway. She lived in an apartment over behind Hopkins, and he drove past my place to get there. When he saw my light on, he dumped his friend rather unceremoniously at her place and came back. There was no question about the shots that were fired at my entry, and, while somebody might be playing games with him, the incident tended to confirm, at least to his satisfaction if not exactly to mine, that somebody was trying to kill him.

I sent him off to bed. I had just finished checking the cat's food dish and water bowl and was on my way up the back stairs when the doorbell rang again. I looked at my watch. Eleven thirty. Not exactly late, but not visiting hours for Miss Manners, either. I continued upstairs to my room, and it rang again. Sighing, I got the gun out of its box and went slowly down the front staircase, realizing that the piece of cardboard covering the place where the window had been shot out of the door would not stop an enraged bunny rabbit. When I got to the door, I said, "Who is it?"

"Annie, it's me. Jack."

CHAPTER 6

I opened the door, and he came in carrying a worn khaki flight bag and his camera bag.

"Don't tell me, you've run away from home."

"Not a bad idea. My flight was cancelled. I think I'm on another one in the morning. Have you heard from Magee?"

I led him to the office and turned on the lights. "Even as we speak he is sleeping upstairs."

"Good. Did he say what was wrong?"

"Only that somebody had tried several times to kill him in the last week. He thinks." I hoped that would satisfy him, but he put his luggage over by the front door and came back to sit on the sofa. I turned the gas logs on again, resigned to more talk.

He looked at the Special Forces book, too, with raised eyebrows. Jack has the funny round face of a Celtic monkey, a shock of unruly brown hair, and matching eyebrows over eyes like clear green pools. He's almost as tall as I am, but so chunky that at thirty-five he still looks like a sturdy little boy in his very first pair of long pants. He has the Slavic soul of the true Celt; dark and low moods alternate with guilty highs. He also has a mind of surprising clarity and focus, considering he went to college during the revolution when nobody was teaching anything but "Ho, Ho, Ho Chi Minh." He has the *National Geographic* photo style down pat, but what he does for his own pleasure are textured black-and-white portraits of any face that interests him, without regard to race, creed, or color. I think he sees the world in layered shades of gray. He wiggled his eyebrows comically.

"Thinking of joining up?"

"If I didn't have to jump out of airplanes I might, just for the rest."

"Jumping out of airplanes is no big deal," he said, echoing Charlie Magee. "There's this big sergeant with a size eighteen combat boot to help you take the first step. After that, it's a piece of cake. Magee was in SF. That's where I met him."

"Well, since you're here, you might as well help."

"That's not why I came."

"I know it's not. I'll see what I can do with Elizabeth while you're gone if you'll tell me about Magee. What's he like when someone's not trying to kill him? How nervy is he? Do you think he's imagining it?"

He wandered into the kitchen and came back with a beer and some brandy. He gave me the brandy and popped the top of his beer. "He's not the type to lose his head. When I first met him, the world was

MARILYNN LAREW

going to hell in a handbasket, and he was cool as ice. When it's quiet, though, he might imagine things, I suppose. He's highly intelligent, and they're the worst kind when they don't have anything to do." He looked into the fire, and for him the room fell away, and it became another time.

"I first met him in February of 1971. I had just finished my degree in journalism at College Park and had convinced the old Washington *Star* that I would be a neat person to send to Viet Nam to cover the dirty war." He grinned to himself. "One summer internship, and I was a war correspondent. I had been in Saigon about long enough to get my foreign correspondent khakis sweat-stained when they sent me north to I Corps to cover the 'Laotian Incursion.'" He snorted. "Vietnamization, ah, yes. I remember it well. The plan was for the ARVN—"

"ARVN?"

"Army of the Republic of Viet Nam. They were supposed to move west along old Colonial Route 9, the road that went past Khe Sanh and Lang Vei, cross the border, and hit hard toward Tchepone, the Laotian town that was a main switching point for the Ho Chi Minh Trail, disrupt the trail, and capture the North Vietnamese headquarters. I went up to Khe Sanh and joined the South Vietnamese First Infantry Division and air assaulted with them into Landing Zone Delta. There was American air support, but no American troops or advisors were to cross the border. There was a nice big fat tank battle between the South Vietnamese US M-60 main battle tanks and the

58

North Vietnamese Ruski T-54s. Snarl up and down, bang. Great pictures. The ARVN lost, of course.

"Some of the air cav troopers headed for Tchepone to make bang, and I went with them. That's the first time I ever saw Magee. He and a bunch of little Rhades—"

"Rhades?"

"That's a tribe. They had been there preparing the banquet for the victorious ARVN troops. A couple of platoons of air cav were all that arrived. Bang. Boom. They blew some stuff, and we split. Great shots, tele-photo lens, of nasty, brutish North Vietnamese in a simple Laotian market town. God, they were small. Almost as small as the Rhades. Magee towered over everybody. I towered over everybody but Magee.

"Back at Aloui, the armor was losing royally. They never did get the hang of infantry fighting in sup-port of armor. As they pulled out, half of the South Vietnamese army tried to crawl on the tanks. At a river crossing near LZ Alpha, they found the North Vietnamese waiting. The lead tank took a hit and got wedged in the crossing. The South Vietnamese aban-doned four M-60s in the stream, and everything else was blocked. Nobody would stand and protect the tanks backed up at the crossing. They just ran and left everything—APCs, tanks, everything."

"They ran? But—"

"But they were supposed to fight the war them-selves? Yeah, they ran. A customary pursuit. All except Magee and his Rhades and some Rangers. They didn't run. The Rangers radioed for help to get the damned tanks out, and the two groups tried to set up some protection while Uncle came to the rescue, but the North Vietnamese were using captured vehicles as machine-gun emplacements. I got my foreign correspondent outfit seriously dirty that day. I was with the ARVN 11th Armored back up the road and had gone up front to see what the holdup was. I was standing on the bank shooting film when the sons of bitches broke behind me and came crawling up my back trying to get across the river. They shoved me into the river, and before I could get up, walked right over my back, firing frantically at anything that moved, ours, theirs, Charlie, whoever. There I was, facedown in the damn river, struggling to get my face or at least my camera out of the water so I could get pictures of our gallant little brown brothers in a typical battle scene, when I felt somebody grab my jacket and pull me up. I was plunked down on the opposite bank, out of the way of the running of the bulls, and when I got the mud screwed out of my eyes, I saw it was Magee. If he hadn't pulled me out of that river, Annie, Elizabeth would have had to find somebody else to blame for world history."

"Surely all of the South Vietnamese troops weren't that bad."

"No, some of them were fine troops. The Marines and the Rangers fought well, but it was difficult to know who to trust. There were South Vietnamese Marines at Khe Sanh, but our Marines strung wire between their position and the South Vietnamese."

"That must have made them feel good."

"Probably, but you can just never tell. After a while the US cavalry arrived and got the tanks shunted aside.

I didn't see Magee again until we were back at Khe Sanh. He and his Rhades were camped at the old Bru CIDG camp at Lang Vei, away from Uncle Sam and far away from the ARVN. I went over to have dinner with them because the 5th Cav had run out of canned peaches, and I knew if I stopped with the ARVN I was going to hose a whole bunch of them down. Besides, Magee's troops were eating woodchuck or jungle rat or something and washing it down with some of the meanest white lightning I ever forced down my gullet." He paused reflectively. "I was drunk some in Nam, but I believe I was drunker those two days at Lang Vei than I ever was before or since. That includes the night I hit San Fran on the way home.

"After a while, the various units got packed up to go home, and Magee and his Rhades got ready to go back to the trail. The last thing he did before I left was take my film out of my camera and hold it up to the light. My editor was not pleased." He laughed and looked up at me under his bushy eyebrows. "Magee's my compadre. Do what you can for him. He wouldn't make anything up." He finished off his beer.

"Why?" Any woman can tell you that the things that bind men together tighter than brothers are wondrously strange.

"Why what?"

"Why did he expose your film?"

"Uncle Samuel was not supposed to have any troops across the river. And the ARVN didn't exactly look like world beaters, did they?" He bent the beer can and set it gently on the coffee table. "Can you give me a bed, Annie? I don't feel like going home."

"Unless you want to bunk with Magee, there's only the couch."

He voted to bunk with Magee, and I pointed him in that direction. I had just taken my shoes off and was contemplating kicking the cat off the bed so that I could get some sleep when I heard loud thumpings from the other bedroom and ran in. Magee was up and out of bed and had Jack flat on the floor and was applying some kind of hold to his neck that left Jack squirming and gagging. I grabbed Magee's shoulders and shook. He loosened his hold, and Jack rolled away. Magee reached back over his shoulder for me and, as I yelled, I felt myself go tail over teakettle and wound up against the far wall.

For a while everybody was doing some fine yelling, but we got it straightened out after Magee woke up thoroughly. I was just explaining and being explained to when the phone rang. It was my next-door neighbor threatening to call the police if I didn't hold it down. I told him the orgy was over and hung up. I could tell I was going to get another letter from the president of the improvement association.

The next morning my shoulder was sore, and I had some trouble getting out of bed without twisting it and making sirens go off. The cat thought it was funny. Cats think human suffering is hilarious. The boys were downstairs drinking coffee and swapping lies. Magee was more cheerful than I had ever seen him, and Jack had temporarily forgotten that he was the root cause of all the evil in the world. It was snowing some and planning to snow more, according to the weather forecast. Jack's plane was scheduled to leave at 1:10, but it had to get here from New York first, and it was snowing worse there. Kennedy was closed. They washed the breakfast dishes, turned on the fire in the office, and settled down with the Sunday paper like good children, while I did some chores at the desk.

The neighborhood handyman maintained that he couldn't put another pane in my front door that day, and possibly not until Tuesday, by which time we would be frozen. The accumulated mail held nothing of interest, despite the fact that I might already have won a million dollars from Publishers' Central, and Mrs. Rowlandson had heard neither from her husband nor her houseman. The three friends of Glenn Rowlandson were not answering their phones, one in Fairfax, Virginia, one in northern Alabama, and one in Los Angeles. No hospital or police force had found the colonel overnight, and the City Room at the *Sun* was talking on the phone. I gave up and joined the paper-reading brigade.

By eleven thirty the radio was chirping about a blizzard, reading cancellations of everything scheduled for the next three days except Baltimore City schools, and Jack cancelled his plane reservation so as not to have to go out to the airport and be told to come back. I called Elizabeth to tell her to come over and put a large piece of beef out to thaw. Along with Miss Marple, I believe gentlemen require red meat.

Elizabeth trekked in with snow in her dark hair and on her eyelashes, looking every bit of eighteen in her ski togs, instead of the serious lawyer two of us knew her to be. It seemed like a good day to sit around the fire, drink, and talk. It was. Magee enlivened a Scrabble game with medical terms, pieces of Southeast Asian dialects that Elizabeth refused to recognize as words because they all had Xs in them, and the pot roast was well received. Elizabeth hardly sulked at all, and Magee spent the night on the couch.

When I woke up Monday morning, the light was glinting off the ceiling, and the world had that secret hush it gets after a good snowfall. It had stopped snowing, and the world looked clean and inviting. No snowplow had violated the accumulation on the street, but several civic-minded folks were out shoveling snow, and their kids were making lovely messes. The world appeared to be on holiday, and I wondered if the liquor store would open up. I was out of gin.

Elizabeth was in the kitchen looking pleased with herself. She poured me a cup of coffee and went on making breakfast for a regiment. The regiment was out in back shoveling snow, having the tactical sense to realize that a car might come in handy whenever the airport decided to open itself back up, although getting out of the alley might present a problem. I looked at my daughter. Her long dark hair was caught up in a ponytail with a scarlet ribbon that matched her running suit, and her face was scrubbed clean, but the roses in her cheeks probably did not come from soap. She was a slim, tidy body, I thought, as she moved gracefully around the kitchen. If only the mood would last. The previous evening was the only time I could remember ever having enjoyed her company without some storm rising between us.

When I left her father she was just beginning school. It was just the wrong time, if there ever is a right time, for her to lose her father. She blamed me for everything, particularly for what happened to her father afterward. Milton was a small-time salesman when I married him, and after I left him, the time became smaller. He slid down the slope from cars through furniture to used recreational vehicles, and he drank, and he gambled, but to her he was always the Prince of the City. She lived with me, and I supported her and took care of her when she was sick and put her through law school, but Milton was the one who bought her the bicycle I couldn't afford and took her out to dinner to grown-up places and courted her as if she were a princess. To do him justice, easier for me now that he was dead, I suppose she was his princess, the one who looked at him with shining eyes and believed every word of his stories long after my eyes had ceased to shine for him. She never sulked for him, and she hardly ever did anything else for me. She was also not too keen on my chosen profession or my occasional contacts with violence.

The final straw had come last December when Milton had been murdered by one of my clients, a tired, unhappy man from Dundalk who had been laid off by Bethlehem Steel and, as a consequence of not being able or willing to do anything else, had taken to beating his wife, Ethel, more than usual. Joe Curtis hired me to find her when she finally ran away. I did find her, and I convinced her to leave him before he really hurt her. While I was away, he kidnapped her and shot her dead in the empty little row house they used to own. Afterward, he came gunning for me and found Milton waiting to try to borrow some money from me. He shot Milton dead too and took off in his car and hadn't been seen since. From what I could tell, Milton's death had been the last of a long list of things that would not have happened to him if I had not divorced him. Things hadn't been too friendly between Elizabeth and me since.

Shortly after that, Jack had thrown her off balance by developing an unliberated desire to get married. I wondered what I could do or say that would make any difference. Whatever I did usually only made things worse between us.

The boys came in rosy-faced from the cold, and we ate a mountain of scrambled eggs, a side of bacon, a loaf of toast, and washed it down with a gallon of coffee. They went back outside to manly work, I did the dishes, and Elizabeth made the beds. If this domesticity kept up, we might wind up having a woman-to-woman talk, and maybe I could persuade her that marriage wasn't all bad. If I could persuade myself first.

Not long before noon, I remembered that Vivian Rowlandson was all alone out at the farm, and as Jack and Magee tracked through the house to shovel the front I went into the office to call to see if she was okay. I had just swiveled around to complain through the hall door about the wet snow they were tracking on the Oriental rug when Magee touched the front door, and a blast blew in the one window I had left in the door.

CHAPTER 7

The sound of the blast brought Elizabeth on the run, but because I was in the office, I got there first. Magee was standing rigidly with his hand still on the doorknob. He had been too close to get anything other than a fat piece of cardboard in his face. Jack, standing farther back, was garnished with glass splinters, and little red flowers were beginning to bloom on his face. For as long as a count of three, the only thing that registered in my mind was the smell of cordite, and then Elizabeth saw the blood on Jack's face and began yelling, and Magee shot a look at me and turned to help Jack. My contribution was to open the door and look out. The vestibule was full of shreds of what looked like cardboard and little metal bits and pieces. There were no other traces on the steps, so it had been put there before the last fall of snow ended. I turned back to the mess in the hall. Magee was fending Elizabeth off with one hand and trying to check Jack's eyes with the other. I took Elizabeth into the office, sat her down in my desk chair, and went for the brandy. She gulped the spirit and hiccupped. Before she could get in her lick, I got in mine. They might be the last calm words I said to her.

"Be quiet, Elizabeth."

She turned on me. "Why, why do these things always happen around you?" she shouted and prepared to throw the glass.

I shrugged. What good would it do? But of course I couldn't resist the siren call of a flippant answer. "It's been months since anybody tried to kill me, Elizabeth."

She threw the glass. It hit the rug and bounced, which was fortunate since there was already enough broken glass on the floor.

"Missed his eyes," Magee said.

"Good," I replied and took over the mopping-up operation. "Look outside," I told him.

"It looks like a shoe box," he said after a minute.

"And smells like gunpowder. Are those bits of a watch? It's time to call the police, before somebody else does."

Jack was beginning to get restive under my face mopping. I gave him the Kleenex and went for the phone. As I touched it, it rang. My neighbor, either inquiring or complaining; I didn't take time to listen. I hoped the president of the improvement association wouldn't have to rewrite the letter.

"Get off the damned phone," I said hotly, "or call the cops yourself." I cleared the line and punched

911. I heard my voice shake a little as I told the dispatcher what had happened.

Elizabeth, calm now, but dead white from anger or fear, handed me the brandy glass and went into the hall to assess the damage to the man she didn't want to marry.

Magee was still standing in the doorway. "Yeah, it's a Timex," he said. "Amateur job."

I looked at him. "Why gunpowder? How would you wire that? And for that matter, why, period?"

"I don't know why, unless it's another attempt at me."

"With a little bit of gunpowder in a shoe box up against my door? How would that get you?"

He shook his head and closed the windowless door. It took the police ten minutes to get there, not bad for the condition of the roads. I yelled at the patrolman to keep off the steps and sidewalk in case there might be useful footprints. Reinforcements would be on the way. My neighbors had long since stopped coming out for my emergencies, but I could see the curtains across the street twitch.

More police arrived soon and began to stand around and look at things. I took the family into the kitchen and fed us all coffee with brandy. The damage to Jack seemed minimal. He sat still while Magee took a couple of slivers out of his face with tweezers. The bleeding had stopped, and he looked no worse than if he had been shaved by an incompetent barber with the shakes. He kept mumbling about his editor. A suspiciously quiet and domestic Elizabeth made more coffee for the policemen when they finished recording the mess outside and began to filter inside where it was warm and there were people to bother. Coffee and questions and sandwiches took up the rest of the afternoon.

For some reason Homer Kruger, the head of the homicide squad, showed up about five to eat a sandwich and listen to Magee tell his story for the fourth or fifth time. Kruger looked more than usually like a former Marine with a weight problem. They didn't like the fact that Magee had not called the police about any of what Kruger called the "alleged attempts" on his life after the first one, which they hadn't believed. He began to get uncooperative, with a decided touch of sullen, after the fifth repetition. And they didn't like that, either.

The members of the bomb squad were new to me. The shift commander, a lieutenant named Proctor, looked about twelve years old, five-foot-eight, and blond, with the tidy body of a swimmer and the crew cut good looks of a lifeguard. He was cool, competent, and polite; they have a course in polite now at the police academy. Homer hadn't taken it. He chewed on his cigarette with his usual rage. He's trying to quit, but the murder rate in Baltimore keeps going up, and he keeps getting called to my house. None of them liked what they heard. Neither did I, for that matter. A small box bomb couldn't be expected to take Magee out unless he picked it up, and even then it would perform like a letter bomb. Damage to hands, face, and eyes—nasty maybe, but not life-threatening.

There were no tracks in the snow either on the sidewalk or in the entry. None of us had even looked out front after Elizabeth arrived. The shoe box could have been placed against the door any time within twelve hours after that. Was it possible that all the attempts were designed only to scare him? If somebody was trying to scare him, it seemed that they ought to tell him why, so he could be properly scared. This one was different from the other attempts on his life. More like the cat. I said so.

"What cat?" Kruger asked in his gravelly voice.

I told him about the dead cat on the doorstep yesterday. Saturday? Yes. Saturday. The day before yesterday. They all trooped out to the garbage can and retrieved the dead cat. I gave them a couple of names that sprang to mind from my case list, and they finally left dissatisfied.

By that time, it was too late for Jack to do anything about Nicaragua but call his editor and relax under Elizabeth's ministrations. She caught me looking at her out of the corner of my eye and turned away, so I went to help Magee, who had swept up the glass and was placing more cardboard in the door windows.

"By tomorrow afternoon they'll know I was a demolitions man in SF," he said.

"I thought you were a medic."

"We're cross-trained. They'll have more questions to ask." He turned to look at me. "If you haven't already asked them."

I shook my head. If he could set bombs, he could set a better bomb than that. In his car, for instance.

Unless—I eyed him again. He wasn't really the kind of man who went to a woman for help. Were we playing Fool the Detective? It wouldn't be the first time some guy hired me because he thought I was dumb. Maybe the whole thing was a charade to fool the fire department. My face must have changed, because he nodded.

"That's what I meant. Mother Magee's angel-faced boy. Stories to fit all situations. Wait until they find out I worked on loan to the CIA. You buy, we lie."

He had turned on the sex appeal again, and my little heart was supposed to go bumpety-bump, I thought grumpily. I decided to trust my client provisionally, but I made a firm resolution to keep an eye on him, especially when he turned on the Irish. I shook my head.

"Who could believe that of you, with a smile like that?"

I went into the office to get organized. He wasn't the only one who needed help. If I was going to work both his case and Mrs. Rowlandson's, I was going to need some troops. Which reminded me that I hadn't finished the call to The Gables to check on my client.

After about twenty rings, Vivian Rowlandson answered the phone. Either it was in a bad place or she wasn't used to doing her own phone answering. Or, I realized as I listened to her voice, she was sloshed.

"I'm simply splendid, Miss Carter. Splendid! See Vivian shovel shit. See her pitch hay. See her shift sacks of grain. See her take care of ten horses. A day of virtuous labor. You don't know where I can get a stable hand, do you?"

The s's were only slightly slurred. After a day of virtuous labor, maybe she was entitled, but she was the one who wanted to keep ten horses. Could I see one small *montagnard* take care of ten horses, a large house, and Vivian? Not to mention Glenn. I hadn't seen any other servant out there. I hung up and tried LA, Fairfax, and northern Alabama again. Still no answer. I settled down to think, but there were too many people in my space for me to think clearly. I wandered into the kitchen. Elizabeth and Jack were thawing something in the microwave. I wandered back into the office. Magee was staring into the fire. I sat down, put my feet up on the fender, and did the same. Fireplaces induce thinking. I thought. The next thing I knew, Magee was shaking me awake. The thawed food was ready to eat.

It turned out to be a chicken with Dijon mustard sauce. There were potatoes and other vegetables and a salad. Looking into the fireplace was not a bad idea. Elizabeth and Jack are good cooks. Elizabeth is slightly better than Jack, who has a tendency to experiments that don't quite come off, like trying to marry Elizabeth.

They had cooked, so Magee and I cleaned up. While he was drying the stuff that doesn't go in the dishwasher, he asked, "What's with you and your daughter?"

Just what I needed. Ann Landers.

"She doesn't like my job, and she's never grown out of the idea that mothers ought to stay home and bake cookies. I was never much of a cookie baker even when I stayed home."

"That's too simple. Maybe you feel guilty about not staying home and baking cookies."

"Amateur psychologist and male chauvinist pig." I tried to say it lightly.

"There aren't too many women who stay home and bake cookies these days," he offered.

"And there still aren't too many who pack a pistol and have the odd bomb or dead cat left on their doorsteps. Maybe she worries about me."

"She doesn't show any signs of wanting to stay home and bake cookies herself. What has she got against marrying Jack?"

"I'm not sure. He thinks my allergy to marriage has rubbed off on her. Maybe he's right, but I can't very well sit down and try to convince her that marriage is a garden of earthly delights and complete fulfillment for man and woman. Somehow I don't think she'd believe me."

"Not if you don't believe it." He put the dish towel on the rack and leaned against the refrigerator, crossing his arms over his chest. "Why don't you believe it?"

"Because my garden of earthly delights had beetles in it. Cut worms. Moles. I don't know." I shifted restlessly. "I'd just as soon not talk about it."

"Maybe you need to."

I finished up at the sink and turned on the dishwasher.

"I'm not sure you, as a two-time loser, are the best person to give me advice about that," I snapped.

"Well, excu-u-use me."

"At least I had the sense not to make the same mistake twice."

"I didn't make the same mistake twice. I made two different mistakes," he retorted.

We were whispering ferociously at each other. His face was black with anger, and mine felt red with same.

"I don't actually like bombs on the stoop, you know, but it comes with the territory."

"Okay, okay." He pushed both hands in front of him, as if to fend me off.

"It's perfectly normal for you to go in harm's way. Socially useful and approved, desirable, even heroic . . ."

"Yeah. I got a lot of thanks when I got home from Viet Nam. That's why they called us 'baby burners.' I probably saved more babies in one sick call or with one well we helped the *montagnards* dig than any of you did by sending checks to Save the Children."

Now it was my turn to say it. "Okay, okay."

We went back into the office, all the good feelings that had developed between us gone. Jack and Elizabeth were sitting close to each other on the couch. She looked strained. He looked as if he had a bad case of chicken pox.

"What did your editor say?" I asked him.

"That I might be safer in the war zone," he answered and gave a sidewise ironic glance at Elizabeth.

"Probably would," Magee contributed. "Who are they to damage a Yanqui newsman when aid to the Contras is such a hot topic?"

"He's been trying to get me on the phone. I got a week's reprieve. The guy who's supposed to write the article is trapped by the snow on Cape Cod. Why would anyone go to the Cape in February?"

"For peace and quiet," Elizabeth snapped. "Let's go home before somebody sets fire to the house."

"On the other hand, without our little bomb, Jack would be stuck in Managua for a week with nothing to do but ogle the lady militiamen." Magee turned on all his black Irish charm for her. "He's been through worse than this on a quiet Saturday night in Saigon."

"Well, I haven't," she retorted sourly, but she couldn't keep a small smile from flickering briefly across her lips.

"You should practice law in the real world for a while, my girl," Jack said as he pulled her to her feet. "You'd soon learn something about the facts of life. Let's go home. I'll give you a short course. With an examination at the end of the hour."

"That's easy for you to say," she replied. "If it's not Magee somebody is trying to kill, it's my mother." Her voice quivered.

He jollied her into her jacket and boots and hustled her out the door.

Work, I thought, that should clear my brain. At least I hoped it would. What with bombs, dead cats, and Magee's black Irish charm, my brain badly needed clearing.

CHAPTER 8

It seemed that I needed Harold again. I often do. Harold is sometimes hard to find and occasionally hard to get along with, but he is a good operative when he's straight. Thin, gray, and wasted, with the posture and complexion of an old-fashioned lunger, Harold likes to dose his troubles with whatever he can find in his herb cupboard, which if the Drug Enforcement Agency doesn't stop showing off, is not going to be much. With supplies down and prices up, maybe he could pry himself out of his apartment and do some work for me. I don't really know much about him, not even his last name. I've heard him answer to Ellis, and he puts Edwards on his W-4 forms, but once when his skin was full of something nice from Colombia, he kept reciting a limerick about a young lady who was hot and what she had and had not got that ended in Harold Eisenstadt. For a small guy he has a bunch of mean moves, and from something he said once, I gathered somebody had sent him to the spook-and-hood school we keep upcountry in Panama. Recently in the line of duty he had suffered a good rap on the skull that had put him in the hospital in Camden, New Jersey. It had caused temporary amnesia but, other than that, he seemed to be okay. With Harold it was sometimes hard to tell. At any rate, he could still follow smoke through a bonfire. Harold could try to get a line on the guy who came out of the window over by Bon Secours. I turned on the office light.

"Why don't you turn that light off?" Magee said sharply. Startled, I looked up from the phone. "Or at least get out of that window." It had been a long day, and I sat there looking stupidly at him. He crossed the room and pulled the draperies across the big window behind me. "Elizabeth's right, you know. If that bomb wasn't for me, it had to be for you. There ain't nobody else home." He touched me on the shoulder. I wanted to shrug his hand off, but I didn't. Or did I want to? Especially since I seemed to be leaning my head against him. Great. Next I would be cooing while he whispered sweet nothings in my shell-pink ear. Mother Magee's angel-faced boy. I shrugged his hand off and called Harold.

He was in and sounded right chipper until I mentioned work, but we got it straightened out eventually, and he promised to saunter down to the medical examiner's office on Penn Street in the morning and have a look at the guy, find out if anybody had identified him, and use some of Magee's money to get a photograph. That took care of one case.

Magee was reading the Simpson book and snorting.

"Read page ninety-nine about the movie," I recommended. "I wonder how many divorces it caused on Okinawa."

He looked up. "Why?"

"As I remember it, the way they got sex into the movie was to have some of the guys 'marry' local 'princesses' for reasons of state."

"Sometimes they did. The 'yards were hospitable in the same way the Bedouins used to be. A girl came with the hooch on long-term lease." He turned back to the book, and I turned back to the fire. I pondered briefly what a local princess might look and smell like, but I figured that the guys probably didn't smell too good by that time either. The world was clearly arranged to suit the requirements of men. I couldn't remember ever reading about a tribe that offered slim young men to visiting lady anthropologists. At least not ones sponsored by *National Geographic,* although there were stories about Margaret Meade.

"Charlie—"

"Don't call me Charlie," he replied automatically.

"Well, for God's sake, why not? It's your name," I asked in exasperation.

He looked up. "C is for Charlie."

"Okay."

"C is for Cong. Charlie is what we called the Viet Cong."

"Oh." I thought about that. "What's your middle name?"

"Ethelred."

"Oh." What kind of an Irish woman would name a son after a Saxon king? "Magee?"

He looked up again.

"I need to get a line on a man who was in Special Forces."

"Why?"

"He's missing from his usual haunts, and his wife wants him found."

"Does he get a vote?"

"When I find him, he does, but he's had blackouts, and maybe he needs to be found. His wife gave me some names, and I can't get hold of any of them."

"Who are they?"

"A guy named Rich Selkirk, who lives in Fairfax, Virginia. A Willard MacIntyre in Los Angeles. Sam Osgood in northern Alabama."

An odd look crossed his face. "Even if you could get them, those guys wouldn't tell you anything," he said. "Selkirk owns a security outfit. I worked for him for a while. He's not a talker. Neither is Sam Osgood. He runs a merc school outside of Birmingham. "Pig" MacIntyre has an import outfit in Los Angeles. Imports Asian art, furniture, things like that. At least that's what he says he imports. He's a salesman; he might talk to you, but he wouldn't tell you anything. What's the name of the guy you're looking for?"

"Glenn Rowlandson. Retired as a light colonel in 1972. Know him?"

"Rowlandson, eh? Yeah, I know him." He didn't sound enthusiastic. He looked down at the book in his hand and put it down on the coffee table.

"Well?" I asked somewhat sharply. I half-regretted losing my temper in the kitchen, but, damn the man, he kept throwing me off balance. I wondered if I was going to have to start pulling teeth again to get information out of him.

"They all four ran together for a while, Selkirk, Osgood, MacIntyre, and Rowlandson, on the SF B team in I Corps. All four of them were connected with the old Bru CIDG camp at Lang Vei." He looked to see if that meant anything to me. It didn't. "The Bru are a hill tribe that lived up in the northwest corner of the country between the DMZ and the Laotian border. Across it, actually. Still do, for all I know. The Civilian Irregular Defense Group was a CIA brainstorm. It was supposed to be a village defense militia to protect loyal villages from Cong infiltration, but it never took very well, except in the hills. We used the Bru for commando raids, for trail intelligence, to try to stop infiltration from the Ho Chi Minh Trail. Lang Vei was down the road toward the Laotian border from Khe Sanh."

That name rang a bell, even after all the years. "The American Dien Bien Phu," I said.

"Right," he said sardonically, "the American Dien Bien Phu, or that's what they wanted us to think. All eyes on the gallant Marines defending that isolated, embattled plateau, while whole Viet Cong regiments were infiltrating into South Vietnamese cities. Those poor damn Bru." He disappeared inside his head to some other place, probably that plateau near the Laotian border.

"Rowlandson," I reminded him after a while.

"Yeah, Rowlandson. Missing, is he? He can stay that way as far as I'm concerned."

"Why?"

"When I was there he was supposed to be up at Corps, but he kept sneaking away and showing up at Lang Vei. He would tag along when we went into Laos on patrol. Just what you want is a major hanging around where he's not supposed to be."

"Can't you tell me about him?"

"I don't know much," he said. "I first met him just before Tet in 1968. I was in an A team in a Bru vill across the border in Laos, about fifteen klicks west of Khe Sanh. Me and a bunch of Bru had been down by the trail . . ."

"Trail?"

"The Ho Chi Minh Trail. We'd been doing some surveillance and disruption. He was supposed to be at headquarters but had snuck out to my vill because he couldn't stay away from the field. He was a pain in the neck in a way. Ranked all of us but he didn't get in the way. He just hung around. Then the North Vietnamese took advantage of the Tet New Year's holiday to attack all over the country. A major surprise, and the Khe Sanh Combat Base was attacked, surrounded on all sides, major artillery and ground attacks. Our air force began around-the-clock bombing, and a stray bomb hit my vill, killing a lot of the villagers and a couple of us. Rowlandson was on the west side of the vill. He and a couple of SF guys took a bunch of survivors and headed farther into Laos, moving toward the trail. Me and the rest of the SF guys took the rest of the survivors toward the combat base. Our story is short. When we reached the combat base, the Marines disarmed us and threw us outside the wire to fend for ourselves." He stopped and his face grew black with anger.

"But why?"

"They didn't trust us. They didn't even trust the Vietnamese Marines stationed with them. Strung wire between the Vietnamese and them. Anyway, most of us survived. Heard later that Rowlandson's bunch had it worse. He had to get about twenty women, children, and old men across the trail to get them to safety. The trail was really five intertwined trails there. They had to move during the day, because nighttime was rush hour on the trail, that and the bombing made it impossible to move at night and difficult during the day. They lost a couple of kids and a pregnant woman, but most of them made it to a Hmong vill, where the people took them in. After they rested, Rowlandson and a couple of SF sergeants headed back to our lines. I was at the fire base when they came in. They had been given up for dead, but they were alive, sort of. Fever, dysentery, parasites, infected leech and insect bites—they were a mess. Rowlandson was slow to recover, so they sent him out to a hospital in Japan."

"What was he like?"

"Rowlandson? Quiet. He wasn't the kind to sit around the fire and tell war stories. I never really thought I knew him. Competent or he would never have gotten those people across the trail, and the three of them would never have gotten back to our lines, but as for feeling he was part of the team, no. He was a loner. He was just *there*, and then he wasn't. Sometimes he just disappeared."

CHAPTER 9

I don't know what time it was, late, anyway, because it was late when I went to bed. I don't even know what woke me, maybe Diva jumping down from the bed. I lay there listening, my heart pounding. Somebody was moving quietly on the stairs. I got up in the dark and reached for the box I keep the pistol in. Still in the dark, I opened the bedroom door slowly and quietly. Before I got it all the way open, silence became unnecessary. Some kind of brawl was going on in the hall. I ran to the head of the stairs and turned on the light. Magee, in jeans and no shoes, was wrestling with somebody. I couldn't get a clear shot, but the light made whoever it was break away and run out the door, followed by Magee in his bare feet. When I reached the door, I heard a car ignition. I joined Magee on the steps and watched as a pair of taillights disappeared around the corner. "Who was it?" I asked.

"Don't know. Heavyset guy driving an old blue Mustang."

We went back inside. Whoever it was had pushed the cardboard out of the right-hand window, reached in, and opened the door.

"You ought to know better than to have that kind of lock in a door with windows. I'm going to nail the damned thing shut," Magee muttered angrily. I persuaded him to put the cardboard back over the window frames instead, and we pushed the heavy mahogany hall table up against the door for the rest of the night. I hoped the neighborhood hardware store would be open early. As we turned to go back upstairs, my foot hit something hard that skittered across the floorboards to come to rest at the bottom step. It was a big automatic, a .45? I said so as Magee stooped to look at it.

"It is. Old sucker, maybe Second World War."

I squatted beside him and looked at it.

"The car was an old blue Mustang, wasn't it?"

"Yeah, why?"

"1968?"

"How should I know?"

"The model where the paint peels?"

"How the hell should I know?"

"I don't suppose you got the license number?"

"Annie, in case you didn't notice, it's nighttime out there," he growled. "What's this all about, anyway?"

I sighed. "A guy named Joe Curtis killed two people trying to get to me, one of them my ex-husband, Milton Babcock, with a .45 and drove off in Milton's blue '68 Mustang. It needs a valve job," I said absently as I looked at my watch. Three thirty a.m. Homer Kruger was going to love me. I went into the office and called a number I knew far too well.

We got to see patrolmen from all three shifts that day. "We're going to raise your taxes," one of them grumbled as we waited. Homer didn't bother to come. The night watch commander did, though. He took the cardboard and the gun and our comments. His were not kind.

"Try to stay out of trouble for a few hours, Annie, while we process this stuff. Or better still, go out of town. Or to another planet."

Instead, we went back to bed and didn't wake up until ten o'clock. Magee went down to the hardware store for glass and a new lock and put them in while I sat in the office, trying to pry my eyes open drinking coffee and eating a chicken sandwich.

Harold called. "They identified the corpse from fingerprints. He's Arthur Ho, a fifty-year-old native of Honolulu. For some reason they're playing it very close to their chests. Kruger's office is saying less than nothing. I wasn't the only person asking about him, so I hung around and followed the guy to a boardinghouse on Frederick."

"What did the guy look like?" I asked.

"Medium height, brown hair, balding, wearing a canvas barn coat and aviator shades. I went back to the morgue and checked his name. He signed the log as Roger Phillips. What do you want me to do now? I got a picture. Shall I check the flophouses?"

"Bring me a copy of the picture, do the flophouses, and call me back this afternoon."

I relayed the information to Magee. "That doesn't explain why he was in that building on Hollins Street," I said.

"I don't know why he was there, but I can make a guess as to why he was in Baltimore."

"Guess."

"When I knew him he worked for the Agency overseeing the collection of the opium blocks in Laos."

"You knew him?"

"Not well."

"Why didn't you recognize him? How could you miss the fact that he was Chinese?"

"It wasn't hard. I wasn't trying to identify him; I was trying to keep him alive. His complexion was a bit sallow, but that could have been jaundice or bad light. His face was swollen, and he had the beginnings of two black eyes, so missing an eye fold wasn't hard, and I hadn't seen the son of a bitch for nearly ten years. Okay?"

I accepted that provisionally, since I hadn't seen the man, but the list of things I had only Magee's word for was growing longer.

He looked at the windows and the new lock. "That ought to hold you."

I thanked him and let him out the back door.

Harold arrived with a copy of Artie Ho's photo just as I was finished dressing to go calling.

"I'll do the places around Hollins Street and work my way west," he said.

I had to go to see Wilson Lee at the Chinese Merchants Association, but first I wanted to have a look at that building on Lipps Lane.

I found a parking place on Warwick and discovered that Magee was right. It was eight stories back there. I walked around the front of the big old loft building. Its soft, crumbly bricks were beginning to show their age. Inside, a staircase back at the end of the hall ran up past the machine shop and all the other stuff. A slightly open door on the fourth floor led to a big room that contained only a bunch of trash in the corners and a wooden table with two chairs. The police had been there and left fingerprint powder all over the place, even on a bunch of Chinese carryout cartons on the table. This must be where Artie Ho fell from. The windows were closed. Magee said all the windows were closed when he looked up after finding Ho's body. He didn't tell me the police had talked to him about Artie. Why not? Before or after he was identified? Before? He didn't identify the man the first time we talked. I dislike clients who don't tell me the whole truth. There was nothing more to see in the room, but I wished I could ask Homer about the fingerprints. Did he know something that would help me? Did I know something that would help him?

A balding man wearing aviator shades was outside the door on the wooden stairs when I left. He looked me up and down. He'd know me the next time he saw me. I returned the favor. He was wearing jeans, a canvas barn coat, and hand-tooled cowboy boots. I wouldn't forget him either. I wondered if he had identified Artie Ho at the morgue.

"What are you doing here?" he demanded.

With my hand under my coat on the butt of my gun, I asked, "What are you doing here?" I started down the stairs. He was still looking at me when I lost sight of him.

Harold pulled into the parking place as I pulled out and waved to me. He handed me a copy of Artie Ho's photo.

"Hang around for a while," I told him. "There's a guy upstairs who sounds like the man at the morgue. Follow him. He's upstairs checking out the room where Ho was probably pushed from."

"Okay."

"Do you know if he identified Ho?"

"No."

The Chinese Merchants Association building is on Park Avenue just down from the Enoch Pratt Central Library, and, since it was lunchtime, all the parking spaces around the Chinese restaurants were full. I had to drive back around a couple of blocks and pay for parking in the garage behind the library. The Chinese Merchants Association building was a large three-story brick structure, the only concession to anything Asian being a small green-tiled canopy over the entrance in the left corner of the first floor. That and a large sign that said On Leong–Chinese Merchants Association in big red letters. After the tong wars in San Francisco, none of the merchant associations used the Chinese word for association—*tong*—on their signs. The building was nothing like as exotic as the

Merchants Association building in DC, which was twice as large and dripping with Oriental decorations. That one stood just behind a large ceremonial gate marking the entrance to Chinatown, the gift of the government of Taiwan. Baltimore's Chinatown was quite small in comparison to DC's; most of the Chinese had moved to the suburbs, leaving only some restaurants and a couple of laundries.

I decided to have lunch at Wong's, the place that serves the best Wor Shu Op in town. That's a delectable Cantonese duck dish that seems to be going out of style in other restaurants. Since I knew Wilson Lee was probably having lunch too, I didn't hurry. It was about one when I paid my bill and went out the door. I was climbing over the pile of yellowing snow at the curb, getting ready to cross the street, when I looked up and saw a balding guy in aviator shades and a canvas barn coat step out of the Merchants Association door. Without looking, I knew he was wearing hand-tooled cowboy boots. I stepped back into the cover of the restaurant's entrance and watched him walk down the sidewalk in my direction and get into a dark green Ford. The sticker on the back window told me it was a rental. That guy gets around, I thought. Roger Phillips?

Wilson Lee, the Merchants Association president, owed me a favor for returning his daughter, a wild child who had gone to live the Back to Nature Life in a commune in Frederick some years ago. By the time I found her, she was dirty and disheveled and coming down off a pot high. She was also pretty hungry and ready to go home. Luckily she wasn't pregnant.

Commune life isn't all it's cracked up to be. I figured if Artie Ho had been in town for any length of time, Wilson could find out about it.

The building's foyer showed about as much Asian influence as its façade did, but Wilson's office was another matter. He sat at a rosewood desk against the wall facing the door, a Ming ink painting of tall forested mountains reaching to the clouds on the wall behind him. A seated statue of the Buddha occupied the corner on the left facing a bank of six windows. Alongside it was a rosewood settee with a scarlet cushion and a low table in front. Wilson saw me and pushed a button on his intercom to call for tea.

We seated ourselves on the settee and did the chatting that comes before tea. I sometimes think that the decline of the Chinese Empire was the result of their incessant necessity to drink tea before any business could be done. Still, it was good tea.

"How's Meiling?" I asked.

He smiled. "She's back in school and doing well. I can never thank you enough for bringing her back."

"I'm glad I could help. A small exposure to commune life will work wonders for the gently reared, but it's good that I found her so quickly. If she had gotten used to it, she might have come to like it. A lot of them do."

He shuddered. "What can I do for you today, Annie?" he asked.

"I'm looking for information about this man." I reached into my pack and pulled out the picture of Artie Ho and handed it to him.

Wilson looked at it for at least a minute. "He's dead."

"That's right. He went out of the window of a building over by Hollins Street the other night. Name of Artie Ho. I'm trying to get a line on him—what he was doing in town, how long he'd been here, that sort of thing." I took another sip of tea. "Know anything about him?"

He sat looking at the picture. "May I keep this?"

"Sure," I replied.

"I'll ask around. Somebody might have seen him."

We stood and shook hands. As I was going out the door, Wilson spoke again.

"You're not the first person to ask about him, Annie," he said.

"That guy who just went out the door?"

"Yes."

"Who is he?"

"He said his name was Roger Phillips." Wilson put a slight emphasis on "said."

"And you didn't believe him?"

"He didn't show me his driver's license." Wilson smiled a tiny smile.

"What did he want?"

"He had a picture too. In it the man was alive. He said his name was Frank Tan, he had disappeared with a large amount of Phillips's money."

"And what was Tan doing in Baltimore?"

"Phillips said he had family here."

"Does he? What good would it do to give you a false name if he wants to find the guy?"

"Perhaps he only wanted to see if I recognized the face? Take care, Annie. This is not a nice man."

"Neither was Artie Ho."

I went back to the office to yell at my client in comfort. Magee didn't answer after ten rings, so I switched cases and called Mrs. Rowlandson.

"You should report both vehicles missing," I said.

"I can't. Why should I?"

"Because when the police find the cars, we may be close to finding your husband and Phi."

"I don't have the license plate numbers."

"Do you have your car registration? You'll find the license number on it as well as the insurance information. Call the insurance company and ask what the license numbers for the station wagon and the MG are and call them in as stolen."

"Miss Carter, I—"

"Mrs. Rowlandson, do you want me to find your husband?"

"Of course I do. I wouldn't be paying you money unless I did."

"Exactly. Now report those cars missing. Do it!"

I wondered if she would. The whole thing was strange, and maybe she was the strangest part of all.

Harold was at the front door.

"I thought I'd come in. I found where Ho was staying, a dump on Lips Lane not far from the place where he went out of the window. I told the landlady I was looking for a room. She had one, so I rented it and went out to get the bag I keep in the car. With a little help, my room key opened Ho's room."

You see why Harold is worth a good deal more than I pay him. "Well?"

"Some dirty clothes, two dirty magazines, and a return ticket to LA for today."

"He didn't intend to be here long. Anything else?"

"Just this." He handed me the envelope with the airline ticket in it. There was a phone number scribbled on the back. I dialed it.

"Billy's Place."

"Wrong number," I said and hung up.

According to the telephone book, Billy's Place was a bar on Pennsylvania Avenue.

"Take the ticket back to his room," I said. "Magee says that Ho used to work for the Agency. Go visit your friend at Langley and see what he is willing to tell you."

"It's likely to be ninety percent bullshit, but he might say something useful. I'll see you tomorrow."

CHAPTER 10

Time to try Magee again. This time I let it ring for thirty rings. Nothing. I was getting worried. Where could he be? I got out the upside down telephone directory and found his address. It wasn't much help. It was a mailbox number on Route 144. I pulled out the map and found that Route 144 paralleled I-70 and those numbers were west of Route 32. It took me a while to get out of the center of town and link up to I-70. I turned off I-70 onto Route 32 and turned north on Route 144. It was going dark when I found his mailbox. The Jeep was standing in the driveway, and there were lights in the house. I took the Maglite from the glove compartment and crunched across the snow to the porch, wondering what I would find inside. Did they finally get him? I shifted the flashlight to my left hand and pulled out my pistol. I climbed the three steps to the porch and pounded on the door with the Maglite. After a few minutes, Magee answered, his hair more disordered than usual. He opened the door wide for me to come in and led me to the right, to a living room where a woman was sitting on a sofa smoothing her skirt and patting down a blonde pageboy.

I could feel my face turning red. Holstering my pistol, I said, "I've been trying to get you on the phone. I was worried."

He grimaced. "As you can see, I'm all right. What do you want?"

"Just something about the case. You can call me in the morning. When you have time."

I turned and stumbled out the door. Well, that was fun. Why the hell didn't he answer his phone? I thought I knew the answer to that. I stopped for Chinese carryout on the way home. I looked at my watch. It was nearly eight. Still time to call the West Coast. I asked directory assistance for the phone number for Willard MacIntyre's import business and stripped the paper from the chopsticks while I was being connected. My General Tso's chicken might be cold by the time I finished.

"Rattan Inc.," answered a perky little voice.

"This is Anne Carter. I'd like to speak with Mr. MacIntyre, please."

"I'm sorry, Miss Carter. Mr. MacIntyre is not available."

I sighed. "Mention Glenn Rowlandson's name."

"I'm sorry, Miss Carter. Mr. MacIntyre is not available. He's out of town."

"When will he be back? It's urgent."

"I can't say."

"It's really urgent that I speak with him."

She sounded a little less perky. "Miss Carter, I don't know when he'll be back. He didn't tell me."

I was really having luck on the telephone today. It was too late to call Fairfax, Virginia, or Birmingham, Alabama. That left me nothing to do but eat my General Tso's chicken and contemplate the number of ways I was going to damage Charlie Magee when I saw him again. I was in the kitchen disposing of the remains of my carryout when the phone rang. I picked up on the kitchen extension.

"Hello?"

"This is Vivian Rowlandson, Miss Carter. The police found the MG. It was at the airport."

I was not terribly surprised. "Have they had any luck finding the station wagon?"

"No. Have you made any progress?"

"I can't get any of his friends on the phone. It's my guess that the station wagon is at the airport too."

"You think they went somewhere together?"

"Perhaps."

"They're gone. You think they're gone. Where?"

Good question.

The next morning dawned bright and early with the sun bouncing off the snow and into my eyes. It didn't get better. I had hardly finished breakfast when I heard a knock on the back door, and Magee walked in. I jerked my head toward the hall and said, "Office." I poured two mugs of coffee and followed him.

"Last night was no problem."

"Well, it was for me." I felt my face getting red again. I slapped his mug down so hard that I sloshed some coffee on the desk. I grabbed a fistful of tissues and mopped it up, throwing the wet tissues into the trash can. "I'm allergic to beautiful blondes. I'm particularly allergic to *young* beautiful blondes. Next time I can't find you, I'll assume that you're rolling in the sheets rather than lying on the floor bleeding to death."

He looked at me over his coffee mug and gave me that black Irish smile. "Okay."

"Watch it," I warned.

It widened into a grin. "What was it that you wanted?"

I tried to remember. "Oh, yeah. I went over to Lipps Lane yesterday and found the room Artie Ho went out of. The police had been there. There was fingerprint powder all over the place, including on a couple of Chinese carryout cartons. The police must have questioned you. You didn't tell me about that."

"They didn't believe me either."

I slapped my hand on the desk. "Don't do that! Tell me about it."

"They just wanted to know what happened. What I saw. I told them what I told you, which wasn't much."

"They must have believed you to some degree, or you'd be in jail. Did they say anything about the fingerprints?"

"No."

"Did they say anything about anything? Anything to give me a hook?"

"No."

My glare made him shift in the chair.

"No. Nothing. Why would they? I was there to give them information, not for them to give me information."

Good point. I changed the subject. "I'm not the only person asking around about Artie Ho. Harold saw a guy at the morgue and followed him to a boardinghouse on Frederick. I saw the same man at the building on Lipps Lane, and he stopped at the Chinese Merchants Association and spoke to Wilson Lee. A balding guy wearing aviator shades and a canvas barn coat. He had a picture of Ho. Called him Frank Tan. He gave Wilson what Wilson thought was a false name—Roger Phillips, the name he used at the morgue. Ever heard of him?"

"No. Maybe he's CIA."

"I sent Harold to talk to his contact at Langley. See what he comes back with. On another front, the cops found Mrs. Rowlandson's MG at the airport."

"No surprise there. Anything on the station wagon yet?"

"Not yet."

"Maybe she knows he didn't have a blackout. He drove away in the station wagon."

I stared at the corner of my desk. How long did his previous blackout last? Or did he really have a blackout? I heard a car accelerate outside.

"Hup!" Magee yelled and fell down sideways.

I followed his example. Three shots rang out, and the window shattered. I gasped in pain.

"Annie! Are you hit?"

I curled up in a fetal position as the pain moved up my arm and across my chest. He crawled over and put his warm hand on my cheek. I leaned into it and then pulled away.

"No, dammit. I landed on my elbow!" I said and started to get up. I heard a car accelerate again, and Magee put his arm across me to keep me from getting up. There were three shots again, and I heard glass fall in the hall. I lay on my back and stared up into Magee's face.

"Pull the phone down," I said.

He did, and I dialed 911. After I gave my address and message, I heard the dispatcher grunt.

"Stay on the line," she ordered.

I put the phone on the floor and looked at Magee.

"The back door's unlocked," he said.

"And my gun's upstairs."

We crawled into the hall. He went for the back door, and I went for the gun. We sat on the steps together, the gun in my hand, waiting. I began to tremble, and Magee put his arm around me. It felt good, and the shakes began to go away. I heard the scuff of shoes on the sidewalk and looked through the broken window of the door. A man was coming up the steps to the entry. I raised the gun. Then I heard a car pull to the curb, and the guy ran, but not from the gun. It was the police. One of them took off after the man, and the other knocked on the door. I unlocked it and let him in. He looked at the glass on the floor in the hall.

"Three rounds here. There are more in the office."

I led him there. He was standing around looking when his partner joined him.

"Got away," he said, breathing heavily.

"What in? Did you see?"

"Old blue Ford."

"Dammit! That's Joe Curtis!" I said.

The cop got out his notebook. "Joe Curtis. How do you know?"

"He killed his wife and my ex, who was here waiting for me. Got away in an old blue Ford. You'd better call Homer Kruger."

The young cops didn't really want to call the head of the homicide squad, so I did.

"Joe Curtis just shot up my house," I told him.

Kruger growled. "I'll be there."

While we waited, I gave the patrolman the information he needed to make his report and made another pot of coffee. Homer made good time, considering he was coming from Fayette Street. He sent the men back on patrol and came into the kitchen. I poured him a cup of coffee and cups for me and Charlie Magee. We sat around the kitchen table. It was almost homey.

"How do you know it was Curtis?" Kruger asked.

"I don't, but your guy said he got away in an old blue Ford. That .45 you took when the guy invaded the house is the gun that killed Milton and Ethel Curtis, isn't it?"

"Yeah, it is. Damn. Nobody ever gets the license number of that car."

I handed him one of the slugs I picked up in the hall. "He's got a new gun. Homer," I said, "one of these days he's going to get me. He was coming for the house this time. If your guys hadn't got here when they did, he'd have gotten in and tried to kill me."

"Tried?"

"I was sitting on the steps with my gun waiting for him."

There wasn't much else Homer could do, and he finally left.

"Take care of yourself, Annie."

"Oh yes, but my luck can't last forever."

That left us nothing to do but sweep up the glass, again. Magee came into the office where I was.

"This time I'm nailing plywood over the door. I don't care what you think."

"Yes, you are. What about that?" I pointed to the office window. It's got to be replaced, or I'll freeze to death."

"Plywood and window. I can do that. You're going to have to keep the curtains pulled. He'll be back."

"I know. Magee, I can't work like this."

He frowned and dumped the swept-up glass in the trash can.

"You can't stay here." He looked at me.

"I have to."

"You don't have to. Come to my place. I've got a spare room, and nobody's tried to kill me in almost a week."

Just what I needed. A tiny bedroom, with Magee radiating sex through the wall. I wondered if Victoria's Secret had a line of lace-trimmed chastity belts. I couldn't stay with him, and I couldn't afford to move to a hotel. I had to stay here, no matter what the danger. It's where I work. Magee took measurements and went to the hardware store, and I sat on the hall steps with my gun. Maybe somehow I could trap Joe Curtis. I wasn't going to be safe until he was behind bars.

Magee nailed plywood across the windows in my beautiful front door. The hall was dark and ugly. Then he went into the office and replaced that window and pulled the curtains. The front of the house was like a cave or a prison cell. I went into the living room and slumped on the sofa. I felt like throwing myself down and crying. My own beautiful house, my safe place, was no longer safe. All because I tried to help a woman out of an abusive marriage. He joined me on the sofa, putting his arm around me.

"You're not coming to my house, are you?"

"Magee, I can't. I don't just live here, I work here. I've got to be here where people can find me."

"People like Joe Curtis."

"That's not fair, Magee. My clients have to be able to find me."

"Well, if you won't come to my place, I guess I'll have to come here. I have to go home and get some stuff. Bolt the back door behind me."

That would be a first. A client protecting me. I went into the kitchen and got out something to thaw for dinner.

After dinner we settled into a weird kind of domesticity. Magee went into the living room to watch a basketball game, and I went into the office to try to figure out what the hell was going on.

Figuring out requires a yellow pad. I got one out and made three lists. My case was simple. Joe Curtis was trying to kill me, and there was nothing I could do about it, unless he came into range. The cops might find him, and if they did that would take care of that. Until they did, I had my head down in a bunker.

Magee's case: I looked at the calendar. Nobody had tried to kill him since Artie Ho was identified. Did that take care of it? If it heated up again, it would have something to do with drugs, because Artie had something to do with drugs.

I went to the shelves next to the fireplace where I keep back issues of *The Baltimore Sun* and picked up editions going back as far as Magee began having trouble and took them to the desk. I found a short report of Artie Ho's death with no details other than his fall. Nothing about the guy invading the ambulance. The *Sun* reporter hadn't heard the story or didn't believe it either.

Glenn Rowlandson's case: according to Rowlandson's wife, he disappeared three weeks ago, driving the family station wagon. She feared he'd had a blackout and was wandering around not knowing who he was. His adopted son, Phi, had recently disappeared in the family MG. That seemed to bother Vivian Rowlandson more than the disappearance of Rowlandson himself. The MG had been found at the airport. The station wagon was probably there too. Why wouldn't Mrs. Rowlandson try to find the station wagon's license number? Did she really want to find her husband? If she didn't, why would she spend money to hire me to find him? There was nothing in the paper about finding a man with amnesia.

There was nothing I could do about my case but wait and see.

Magee's case seemed to be in abeyance. I had to wait and see on that one as well.

The only one I could work was the Rowlandson case. Rowlandson probably wasn't in town. He wasn't in the morgue. He was not in any of the hospitals. He and Phi were probably together, but where? Rowlandson had no friends in town. Mrs. Rowlandson had given me three names: MacIntyre in Los Angeles, Rich Selkirk in Fairfax, Virginia, and Sam Osgood in Birmingham, Alabama. I looked at my watch. It was too late to call Selkirk in Virginia. I might get hold of Osgood in Alabama, though, and I should try MacIntyre again as well.

I flipped open my notebook to find MacIntyre's phone number and dialed it. Miss Perky was still at work.

"Rattan Inc.," she chirped.

"This is Anne Carter again. I'd like to speak with Mr. MacIntyre."

She toned the perky down. "Miss Carter, Mr. MacIntyre has still not returned to the office."

"Can you tell me—?"

"No, I can't. He doesn't always tell me where he's going or when he's coming back, and I just don't know." With that she hung up, somewhat sharply.

Strange behavior for a businessman. I called directory assistance and got connected to the Los Angeles area Better Business Bureau. They had no complaints about Rattan Inc. on record.

"Is there a furniture dealers' association in town?"

"Let me see," the woman said. After a few minutes she came back. "Yes, there is." She gave me the name and address and phone number, and I thanked her.

Next stop was the Furniture Dealers Association. They had never heard of Rattan Inc. Even stranger behavior for a businessman. I began to wonder what Rattan Inc.'s business actually was.

CHAPTER 11

I tried directory assistance for Sam Osgood in Birmingham and got a number for Tactical Training Inc. and what sounded like Osgood's home number. I took down the number for Tac Training and asked the operator to connect me with the home number. A woman answered the phone.

"Is this Mrs. Osgood?" I asked.

"Yes."

"This is Anne Carter. I'd like to speak with your husband about a friend of his who is missing."

"Missing? Who's missing?"

"Glenn Rowlandson."

"Glenn? But he was just here."

"Mrs. Osgood, I need to talk with your husband, please. It's urgent."

I heard her drop the telephone receiver and call her husband. It was a minute before he picked up.

"Hello? Who are you? And what's this about Glenn?" Osgood's voice was a pleasing baritone.

"My name is Anne Carter, Mr. Osgood. I'm a private investigator in Baltimore. Mrs. Rowlandson has asked me to find her husband, Glenn. He's been missing for almost three weeks, and she's afraid he's had a blackout or something has happened to him. She doesn't know where he might be. She gave me your name as a friend. Your wife says he's visited you recently?"

"Yes, Glenn was here last week. Stayed for a couple of days. He comes to visit sometimes, you know?"

That was during the time Mrs. Rowlandson said he was missing. "Does he? Did he say where he was going after he left you?"

"No. I thought he was going home."

"He hasn't arrived, and his wife's worried about him. Can you think of anywhere else he might've gone? Any other friend he might've gone to see?"

"No, unless he went to see Rich."

"That's Rich Selkirk in Fairfax, Virginia?"

"Yes. Glenn and Rich and I were in Viet Nam together. Don't go to any of the reunions, but we visit occasionally."

"Mr. Osgood, how did Mr. Rowlandson seem? Did he seem okay? Healthy? Not confused or anything?"

"Glenn hasn't been healthy since the end of the war. All that time in the jungle didn't do him any good, and every once in a while he comes down with malaria or the parasites kick up again. He didn't seem much different this time. A little tired, but that's normal with Glenn. I know he said he was going home."

"And you can't think of anyplace else he might go besides Fairfax? Los Angeles? Would he visit Willard MacIntyre?"

"'Pig?'" He sounded startled. "No, I don't think so. They were never friendly. Where did you get MacIntyre's name?"

"His wife gave it to me. Said he was a friend."

"I don't know why she'd do that. Glenn would be more likely to shoot him than visit him. They got across each other upcountry in a big way one time. MacIntyre was almost twice Glenn's size, but I had to pull Glenn off of him. He was going to work on him with his knife."

"What was that about?"

"A woman. 'Pig' would never take no for an answer. He was trying to mess around with one of Glenn's people."

"Was it personal with Rowlandson?"

"No, he was just protecting the woman. A lot of the guys thought the women were fair game."

"Do you think he might have stopped to see Selkirk on the way home? Can you give me Selkirk's phone number?"

"I guess he might have. Wait a minute." I heard the sound of paper rustling, and he gave me a 703 number. When I dialed it, nobody answered, and there was no answering machine.

I found Magee in the living room reading the Simpson book about the Special Forces.

"Well?" I asked.

"Not bad," he replied.

I was just thinking about going to bed when Harold called me from DC.

"My CIA contact wouldn't tell me much, but he did tell me that Arthur Ho isn't working for the Agency anymore. He's working for a guy named MacIntyre, a furniture importer in LA. In fact, they were following him, but he slipped the leash. My contact has no idea what he might be doing in Baltimore. What do you want me to do now?"

"Come back and pick up that Roger Phillips guy and try to figure out what he's up to."

"Will do."

The next morning we had bagels. We were just like an old married couple. He had the sports page, and I had the front section. This was going to get on my nerves very soon. One of the things I like about my life is the solitude. Not that he was making any noise, but he was eating a lot of the cream cheese.

The world hadn't improved any, and I was just about to toss the paper when I noticed something unusual on page four among the shootings and robberies. A man with a Chinese name had been found floating in the inner harbor. I don't think I had ever seen a Chinese person in the crime news before. He'd been shot. It was probably nothing, but I called Wilson Lee.

"Who is Samuel Chau Wong?" I asked him.

He cleared his throat. "A recent arrival from the West Coast."

"LA, possibly?"

"Yes."

"As was Artie Ho. Have you found out what he was doing in town?"

"No, I haven't, and I don't think I'm going to."

"Wilson, you must have some less-than-fragrant contacts. This is important to a case I'm working. Try again. Try harder."

Magee emerged from the sports pages. "What?"

"A Chinese man, recently arrived from the West Coast, was found floating in the inner harbor yesterday. Shot."

"Sounds like a Triad kill."

"Triad?"

"A Chinese criminal gang. That's what they call Tongs in China."

"What is a Chinese criminal gang doing in Baltimore?"

"Good question. They move a lot of drugs in China. In the US too, probably."

"I wonder if Baltimore's does."

"Baltimore's what?"

"The formal Chinese name of the Chinese Merchant's Association is On Leong Tong."

"And two Chinese men from out of town have recently been killed in Baltimore?"

"Exactly."

I thought for a moment and then went to the stack of papers. Did I remember an unusual number of shootings recently? I did. Seventeen in the last two weeks to be precise. I got out the map. Nine were along the Pennsylvania Avenue corridor, and eight were down by the docks.

I reached for the phone and called the number I knew only too well.

"Homicide, Kruger."

"Anne Carter, Homer. Got a question for you."

"Not a body?"

"No."

"Not a shot-out window?"

"No."

"Ask."

"Does Tyrone Black's Pennsylvania Avenue Gang still run the heroin trade in Baltimore?"

"Yes."

"And they get their supplies from New York?"

"Yes."

"Any local boys trying to muscle in? There appear to have been a lot of shootings recently."

"Yeah."

"Who's running the docks now?"

"Willy Reid."

"I thought he was inside."

"He is," Kruger growled.

"Ever had any West Coast guys try to move in?"

"No. They'd be up against the whole East Coast mafia."

"You remember Artie Ho?"

"Who?"

"The guy who came out of the window over on Lipps Lane?"

"Oh, yeah. What about him?"

"He used to work for the CIA. I hear he was big in heroin during the Vietnamese war."

"And?"

"And I hear the guy who was pulled from the harbor yesterday is also from the West Coast."

Homer went silent, and I could hear somebody tapping on a typewriter behind him. "Why would West Coast guys try to move into Baltimore heroin?"

"Better product and lower price? Perhaps they're not. I can't figure out why either would be dead in Baltimore, unless they'd crossed somebody big-time."

"It's a thought. You stay out of it."

"You bet, but it may be connected with Magee's problem."

"Remind me."

"Somebody's been trying to kill him?"

"Oh. The guy with the imagination."

"Goodbye, Homer."

Magee poured himself another cup of coffee. "He still doesn't believe me, does he?"

Magee cleared the table, and I went to the office to try Rich Selkirk again. He still didn't answer, and he still didn't have an answering machine. Magee walked into the cave that was my office with the curtains closed.

"You say you used to work for Selkirk's outfit? What is its name? Nobody's answering at the house."

"Selkirk Security."

I got the number from directory assistance and dialed. The receptionist wasn't quite as perky as MacIntyre's receptionist, but the answer was the same.

"I'm sorry. Mr. Selkirk is not available."

"My call is urgent. Tell him it's about Glenn Rowlandson."

"I'm sorry, Miss Carter. Mr. Selkirk is out of town."

"When do you expect him back?"

"I really can't say."

"Look, this is urgent. When is he coming back?"

"I'm sorry. I can't tell you when he's coming back. I don't have that information."

Magee came into the office with the rest of the newspaper and sat down on the couch.

"Selkirk's out of town too. Funny, neither he nor MacIntyre told his staff when he was coming back. How long did you work for him?"

"About a year."

"Why did you quit?"

"It was boring. All I did was check people through metal detectors. Once in a while there was a bodyguarding job or a transfer of a bunch of money or important packages. Security isn't all that exciting."

I smiled at him. "And you require excitement?"

He grinned back. "Yeah. Life was so boring before I met you."

I settled down to do some book work. Private detecting is not all that exciting either. It comes with a bunch of paperwork. I prepared two bills on which payment was overdue. I used my cute rubber stamp with red ink threatening to turn them over to a collection agency. That would cost me a percentage; I'd let them run for another month, but it was bad form to let a client stiff you. I'll bet Sam Spade never had that problem. I turned to writing reports for the client files. I opened a file for myself and recorded Joe Curtis's various attacks on the house, ending with yesterday's shooting spree. I sat back and looked at the fireplace. There was no way I could find him. If the police didn't grab him, I might be dead.

I caught up on Magee's case. "Do you realize that nobody's tried to kill you in over a week?" I asked him. "Not since Artie Ho was identified. Did somebody want to prevent you from identifying him? I haven't done all that much work on the case."

"You went over to Lipps Lane."

"And saw Wilson Lee at the Merchants Association."

"And made some long-distance calls."

"Those were more about Glenn Rowlandson than about you. In return, you are currently bodyguarding me. I think I owe you."

He laughed. "I'm not sure you can afford my hourly rate."

I put the files in the inbox. "When are they going to have your hearing?"

"They've already had it. They still don't believe me. I'm on a month's suspension."

"And you didn't think to tell me about this?"

"Things kept happening." He went back to the newspaper.

I had to get away from the cave, but I live in a row house, so the current living room has no windows, and I thought I might scream if I couldn't look out of a window, so I went upstairs to my bedroom and sat on the chair beside the window. Mrs. Rowlandson thought he might be wandering around in a daze not knowing who he was, but Sam Osgood said he'd visited them the previous week. Osgood thought he might be going to see Rich Selkirk. I wondered if Rich Selkirk really was out of town. Fairfax was not all that far. I looked at my watch and saw that I had plenty of time to get there and back before dark.

Downstairs, I picked up my coat.

"Where are you going?" Magee asked.

"To Fairfax to see if Rich Selkirk is really out of town," I replied.

"Not without me you're not."

"Magee—"

"Your body doesn't go anywhere without its guard."

It seemed simpler to take him than argue.

All of Fairfax was upscale, but the neighborhood where Rich Selkirk lived in was upscaler. A five-bay, two-story colonial that had been around for a while stood on a couple of acres. The driveway led around back to a three-car garage. A peek through a window in the door showed all three cars in residence. I drove back to the street and parked at the curb.

"Three cars in the garage."

"Maybe he took a taxi."

"You're a big help."

A chubby guy in blue jeans and a sweatshirt answered the door in his bare feet. His brown hair was retreating faster than he could comb it over his skull, and a pair of dull gray eyes looked at us through bifocals. They sharpened when he saw Magee.

"What the hell. 'Don't call me Charlie' Magee."

He opened the storm door and offered his hand.

"How's it going, Rich? Your office says you're out of town." We moved inside before Selkirk could object. He moved back in the face of both of us.

"This is Annie," Magee said. "She's looking for Glenn Rowlandson."

It didn't look like he was going to offer us a chair or a cup of tea.

"What makes you think I know where he is?"

"Sam Osgood," I said. "He said Rowlandson was coming here when he left Birmingham last week."

"What's it to you?" he asked belligerently.

"Now, Rich, play nice," Magee said and moved closer to him.

"Mrs. Rowlandson's looking for him. She thinks he's had a blackout, but Sam Osgood said he looked pretty good last week. Where is he?" I asked and moved closer to him too.

Selkirk shoved back at us. "Get the hell out of here. I haven't seen Rowlandson and wouldn't tell you if I had."

I looked at Magee. "Do we believe him?"

Magee smiled. "I wouldn't believe him if he told me that the sun comes up in the east."

"He doesn't look too trustworthy to me either. Do we shove him over and search the place?"

Selkirk's face grew bright red.

"That wouldn't be polite," Magee said and turned on his heel.

"You're right," I said and followed him out the door.

Back in the car I asked, "What did that get us?"

"Not much. Except we know he's not out of town."

"You're the one who knows him. You think he's seen Rowlandson?"

"I couldn't tell."

Well, it got me out of the office, anyway.

CHAPTER 12

I was thinking of sending out for pizza when I heard somebody pounding on the back door. It was Elizabeth.

"What's the back door doing locked? Why is Magee here?" She put a bag of groceries down on the kitchen table.

"He's protecting me."

She looked at me sharply. "He's protecting you?"

"Joe Curtis shot the place up last night."

"*Mother*—"

"Don't start with me, Elizabeth. I'm tired. All I did was try to free a woman from an abusive marriage, something even you might have done. Curtis has killed his wife and your father and is gunning for me." Tears came to my eyes, and I wiped them away angrily.

"Mom." Elizabeth put her arms around me and hugged me. I rested my cheek on her shining hair.

"And if the cops don't pick him up, he'll get me. My luck can't last forever."

She hugged me harder.

"What's going on here?" Magee asked from the door.

I stood up. "Just a non-private-eye moment," I said.

Elizabeth blew her nose and unpacked the groceries. "I only brought two steaks. I didn't know Magee was here."

"Cut one third off of each steak," Magee said.

"I'm not hungry," I said.

"You have to eat something," he said. "You need to keep your strength up."

I turned on him. "If you're going to be right all the time, it's going to have a bad effect on our relationship." I walked into the hall and leaned my head on the newel post.

"My mother is *frightened*?" I heard Elizabeth ask.

"She'd be a fool if she wasn't," Magee answered.

And I'm not a fool, I thought. Magee came into the hall and put his arm around my shoulders. I stood there, feeling his warmth, until I heard the phone ring in the office. I walked away from him and answered the phone. It was Vivian Rowlandson.

"Miss Carter, somebody's broken into the house!"

"Was anything taken?"

"No. I mean, I can't tell."

"Call the police."

"No. I want you to come!"

"Mrs. Rowlandson, call the police. It will take me an hour to get there."

"Come. Get here as fast as you can!"

"How did they get in?"

"I don't know. I was at the grocery store. When I got back the kitchen door was open."

"Get out of there," I said. "Get out of there now. Go and sit in your car with the engine running and the doors locked. If you see anybody, leave! I'll be there as fast as I can get there." I went into the kitchen, where Magee was making a salad and Elizabeth was preparing to grill the steaks. "Put the steaks away, Elizabeth. Magee, somebody's broken into the Rowlandson place, and Mrs. Rowlandson will not call the cops. I need to get out there as fast as I can."

"Mother—"

"Don't start, Elizabeth. Just put the steaks in the refrigerator and go home. I'm not leaving you in the house alone."

I heard her mutter something that started with "you always . . ." She didn't finish. She just wrapped the steaks, put them in the refrigerator, and went out the back door, slamming it behind her. I took my coat off the hook by the back door.

"I'll be back."

Magee took his coat from the hook next to mine. "Where your body goes your bodyguard goes."

"You'd better have my spare gun, then." I went upstairs and got the .38 revolver and a box of ammunition and took them down to him. "I don't have a holster for it."

He snapped the revolver open and loaded it. "That's okay," he said and stuck it in his belt.

"Your choice," I said.

We took my car, and I began working my way north on Charles to get to the beltway. The traffic lights on Charles are designed to drive a person mad or create traffic jams. Traffic was particularly bad around Johns Hopkins University, but after we got past that chokepoint, things cleared up. The beltway, of course, was still suffering from rush hour, but we eventually got to Reisterstown Road and turned west into new congestion and traffic lights. It was almost exactly an hour when I turned onto The Gables drive and drove up its one plowed lane. Mrs. Rowlandson's car was running, and the windows were steamed up. How could she see anybody coming? I hit the horn three times, and she rolled down a window.

"Stay put while we check the house," I ordered her.

We went through the open door to the kitchen and through it to the hall. Magee was staggered by the decor. He shook his head in wonder and turned to the right to check out the living room. I turned to the left to check out the dining room and her sitting room. We met back in the hall.

"It's clear," I said.

"Yeah, it is."

We went cautiously up the stairs and down the hall, checking those rooms. They were clear too.

We went back down to get Mrs. Rowlandson.

"Come inside," I said. "This is my associate, Charlie Magee." She nodded to him but didn't offer her hand. I guess an associate is too low on the pecking order to require courtesy.

"I need you to tell me what's missing."

We walked through the dining room and her sitting room.

"I don't see anything missing," she said.

In the living room, she saw nothing missing either. "Wait." She went to the mantelpiece and looked at the cluster of photographs in silver frames. "No, I thought the picture of Glenn's mother was missing, but it's here." She picked up an oval frame from the last row and handed it to me. It showed a pleasant-looking woman with a soft face surrounded by white hair. "Maybe Phi moved it the last time he polished the frames?" she said uncertainly.

Nothing seemed missing on the first floor. We went upstairs. Mrs. Rowlandson took us through her room and shook her head. "No, nothing."

We moved on to Glenn Rowlandson's rooms.

"I'll leave you here," Mrs. Rowlandson said and left us, almost hurrying away.

Magee and I went into Rowlandson's bedroom.

"What's that all about?" he asked.

"She doesn't like to be in his rooms. She stayed for a while when I searched them before, talking as fast as she could. She finally left. She does talk a lot, but I can't get a fix on what she thinks of her husband. She recited his 201 file in detail, but when I asked her about more personal things, she had nothing to say."

"That and separate bedrooms says that they're not all that close. He is a hard guy to know. Quiet and withdrawn with us. He talked enough to the locals."

"That's about what she said. It must be fun, the two of them rattling around in this huge place."

"There must be a lot of money somewhere," Magee said.

"I think it's from her family. This place belonged to them."

Nothing that I could remember seemed missing from his bedroom; we moved on to his study. It was immediately obvious that there was something missing from there—the Chinese scroll painting. I said so. "It was lovely, a painting of a line of men on horseback riding alongside a river that was overshadowed by huge mountains. Must be worth thousands of dollars."

I didn't see anything else missing, but I sat down at the desk and opened the top drawer. There was no checkbook there. I was certain there had been a checkbook there before. I looked into the bottom side drawer where there were a number of files hanging. I pulled out the file with monthly statements of his investments from Alex. Brown & Sons, the investment bank. The last one showed a balance of one hundred dollars. I sat back in the chair and reached for the file of his bank statements. The only things there were his army pension, Social Security, and a deposit of fifty thousand dollars from Alex. Brown, which he withdrew by a check made out to cash. I called to Magee, who was looking at books on the shelves.

"Magee, look at this."

He came and looked over my shoulder.

"He's sold his whole portfolio."

"What's he done with it?" Magee asked.

"Put it somewhere else, obviously."

"Then he's not having a blackout. He's running away."

"And either he or Phi was here today. That scroll and the checkbook are all I can find missing."

I took some of the financial statements, and we went downstairs to find Vivian Rowlandson in her sitting room. She had started a fire in the fireplace and was looking into it. I showed her an Alex. Brown statement and one of the bank statements.

"You knew he didn't have a blackout, didn't you?"

She nodded.

I sat down on the sofa beside her, and Magee leaned against the doorframe, arms crossed over his chest.

"Why did you lie to me?"

"I need for you to find him."

"You didn't give me much to work with," I said.

"I don't have much. I didn't see those statements, but I knew he was gone, especially when Phi left. They're never apart." She gave a ragged little sob.

"Vivian, I think I've done all I can."

"Please, you must find him."

"He's left you. Why is it so important that you find him?"

"Because of the will."

"What will?"

"My father's. My father left everything to Glenn. I only inherit after Glenn's death."

I raised my eyebrows. "An unusual will."

She shrugged her shoulders and picked up her jade cigarette holder. She took a cigarette from the box on the table and tried to put it into the holder and light it. The attempt to produce the kind of airy insouciance she had exhibited the last time I was at The Gables was undercut by her trembling hands. It was painful to watch.

"Do you know why he left?"

She threw the cigarette holder in the table. "Just find Glenn for me, please," she asked. "I haven't got enough money to live on. You have to find him."

If she didn't have enough money to live on, she didn't have enough money to pay me.

"Magee, will you go upstairs and look in the desk for an address book?"

He pulled away from the doorframe and went back into the hall.

"I'll need some more information from you. I'll need to talk to the lawyer who drew the will up and to Colonel Rowlandson's doctor. I've got his broker's name here on this statement. Call tomorrow, please, and get them to see me. At the moment I have no leads. If I can't get any from them, I'll have to give up. In the meantime, list his station wagon as stolen. There is no point in talking to the people in the Missing Persons Bureau. If they do any investigating at all, they'll find out what I just did—that he left voluntarily, and there's no law against that."

Magee came in with an address book, and we left without saying much more, but I did tell her to be sure to throw the deadbolts after we left.

We threaded our way back on Reisterstown Road to the beltway, around the beltway to Charles, and down Charles to Twenty-Fifth Street.

"What did he do with the money?" Magee asked.

"I don't know. Opened new accounts? Why would he do that? They were in his name. She couldn't touch them."

I stopped at a McDonald's near the Hopkins campus. I was hungry enough to eat a Big Mac.

"Do you want anything?" I asked Magee.

"No. There are steaks in the refrigerator. Let's go home. It's not very far."

I drove down the alley behind the row of houses; when I got to my place, I saw the back light was off. I had left it on.

"Is he inside?" I asked.

"Don't know. Let's go around front."

I parked in front of the house and gave Magee the Maglite. We drew our guns, and I unlocked the front door. He kicked it hard enough for it to bang against the wall, and we went cautiously inside. I turned on all the lights and we cleared each room. Nothing. But the back door was unlocked. We locked it. We went cautiously upstairs and down the hall checking the upstairs rooms. Nothing there either, except one worried cat. I took her with us downstairs to the kitchen and got out the gin.

The light on the answering machine was blinking when we went into the office. It was Harold.

"Annie, unless he's on foot, he stayed inside all day. His rental car hasn't been moved from the place it was parked last night. It's kind of hard to stake this place out. There's a bunch of foot traffic, and the cops patrol regularly. I've had to move several times, and

I'm beginning to get funny looks, so I'm going home. Let me know what I should do next."

I called Harold back. "Go get a room in his boardinghouse. If you can't watch Phillips from the outside, you can watch him from the inside."

"Okay. What about the airline ticket?"

"Hold that. Was there any indication that the police had been in Ho's room?"

"No."

"Then they don't know where it is. Forget it for the moment."

"Okay."

I was sitting in the chair by my bedroom window, my heels up on the edge of the chair with my forehead on my knees when I heard the door open. I smelled coffee.

Magee stood in the doorway, a mug of coffee in his hand. "What's wrong?" he asked.

I straightened up and wiped the tears from my face. "I'm trying to get up enough nerve to go downstairs into the cave."

He handed me the coffee. "It's necessary."

"I know it is," I snapped. I drank some coffee. "It's just that being confined is really getting to me. Magee, I feel like I'm in a box. I need to walk free."

"This will be over soon," he said.

"Yes." I finished the coffee. "One way or another."

CHAPTER 13

Archibald Withers, of the firm of Withers, Withers, and Hartman, had his office in an old-fashioned midrise building on Reed Street near Charles. His reception room was presided over by a middle-aged woman wearing tortoiseshell cat's eyeglasses. I sent my card in with Glenn Rowlandson's name written on the back, and Magee settled down on the sofa with the choice of *Architectural Digest* or golf or sailing magazines. Having been warned by Vivian Rowlandson, Withers was willing to see me. Withers's office was as professional as dark wood paneling and shelves full of law books could make it. He rose to shake my hand, a tall middle-aged man with short but not cropped brown hair and brown eyes. His restrained pinstriped suit with narrow lapels and a vest told me his hourly rate was high, and the framed diplomas on the wall told me he was Princeton University and University of Maryland Law School, like all the other classy attorneys in town

"Coffee, please, Mrs. Shields," he said. He ushered me to a leather couch and took the leather armchair next to it. He looked at my card. "I've never met a private eye before," he said with a roguish twinkle in his eyes.

Was he going to hit on me? "It's not as exciting as TV would have you believe," I replied.

"Are you armed?"

Mrs. Shields arrived with the coffee tray, and we sugared and creamed.

"Are you armed?" he repeated.

"Yes, I am."

"Do you expect to be in danger here?" The roguish gleam was back.

"Not here, Mr. Withers, but there's a man who's trying to kill me, so I'm armed."

"Why is he trying to kill you?"

"Because I tried to help his wife."

"And will you shoot him?"

"If necessary." I put my coffee cup on the table. "Mr. Withers, I'm here to ask you about Walter Archer's will."

"I didn't draw it, Miss Carter. My father did. We've taken care of the Archer family's business for three generations. My father understood the situation and made that will as tight as a drum. If Mrs. Rowlandson is thinking about challenging it now . . ."

I ignored that. "It seems extraordinary to me that Archer would leave his estate to his son-in-law rather than to his daughter."

Withers finished his coffee. "I don't know how much I can tell you."

"I understand that, but Colonel Rowlandson has disappeared, and Mrs. Rowlandson has no money. I need to understand that will."

Withers put his elbows on the chair arms and steepled his fingers against his lips. Then he clasped his hands over his tummy. "Miss Carter, you need to know something about the Archer family to understand the situation. Mrs. Rowlandson's mother, Margaret Butler—they called her Daisy—was a pretty thing, the belle of the 1930 Bachelors Cotillion, and Walter Archer carried her off and married her. The problem was that they were ill-suited. Archer was a stockbroker, middle-aged, staid. He had no use for speakeasies or jazz. Daisy was a bright young thing, loved to party. She was the girl that the Charleston was created for. They lived in the Archer townhouse, a brownstone in Mount Vernon Square, where Archer's mother also lived. The elder Mrs. Archer seriously disapproved of Daisy. She would have disapproved of anybody Archer married, of course, but Daisy . . . She just couldn't stand Daisy. After a couple of years Daisy had not produced an heir, and things in the household got worse. By that time, Archer was tired of partying, and Daisy went out without him. After the elder Mrs. Archer died, Daisy thought she would become the mistress of the house, get rid of the dusty velvet draperies and heavy carved furniture, and decorate the house in a modern, jazzy way." He shot a sharp look at me, and I nodded. I could tell what was coming.

"But that was not to be. Walter wanted the house kept the way it had been when his mother was alive. Daisy partied more furiously."

"How do you know all of this, Mr. Withers?"

"My father told me most of it. I've always thought it sounded like a novel by F. Scott Fitzgerald. Anyway, Vivian was born, a pretty little blue-eyed baby." He looked at me, and I looked back.

"And both Archers' eyes were brown?"

"And the Archers' eyes were brown. In a cold rage, Archer sold the townhouse over Daisy's objections and moved them permanently out to The Gables."

"And they all lived miserably ever after," I said.

"Exactly. Daisy, her partying days over, soon faded and died. Growing up, Vivian did everything she could do to please her father, but nothing she could do could earn his love. When she grew older, she became a party girl just like her mother had been, and that only made her father colder. She, too, was the belle of the ball at the Bachelors Cotillion."

"And then she married Glenn Rowlandson, an army officer from a very good Anne Arundel County family," I said.

"And then she married an army officer from a very good Anne Arundel County family. Walter always liked Glenn, although because of his military service, Glenn was rarely at home."

"Which left Vivian alone with her implacable father."

"Precisely. Shortly before he died, Archer made that will, hoping that Vivian would never lay her hands on a penny of his money."

I sat back on the sofa. He was right. It sounded just like F. Scott Fitzgerald. What could be done? "Mr. Withers, Vivian has nothing to live on. She can't even mortgage the property. She doesn't own it. If I can find Colonel Rowlandson, is it possible that he can make over some money to her?"

He mulled that over. "I'd have to do some research on that, Miss Carter."

"It's Rowlandson's property. Surely he can dispose of it any way he likes."

"I'd have to read the will. I've forgotten its exact wording."

That didn't sound promising. I knew that the only thing left was The Gables, and short of his making it over to her entirely, there was nothing he could give her. He'd cashed it all out and put it somewhere. Poor Vivian. Screwed twice. And all for being her mother's daughter.

Withers and I shook hands, and he escorted me out of his office. When I came into the reception room, Magee was reading *Architectural Digest*.

"I'm thinking of buying a Frank Lloyd Wright house in Kansas City," he said as we left.

"Be careful," I said. "He built all of them to his own scale, and you're considerably taller than he was."

We needed to grab a bite of lunch before seeing the broker at Alex. Brown. I thought of going to the Woman's Industrial Exchange, but somehow I didn't see Magee among ladies wearing hats and eating tomato aspic. Pity. Their softshell crabs were wonderful. We stopped for a burger and fries.

"You mean she was more or less disinherited because her father thought she wasn't his daughter?" Magee asked.

"That's what Withers said. And now she hasn't got a nickel."

"Which means she can't pay your bill."

"Which means she can't pay my bill."

"The sins of the mothers . . ."

West Baltimore Street was as crowded as usual. I had to scoot under the nose of a bus to get into the right-hand lane to turn onto South Street to get to the Alex. Brown building. This caused outraged honking in two lanes. The building was a solid two-story Classical Revival structure of red brick with stone quoins, a substantial, respectable place in which to leave your investment portfolio. At the reception desk, I asked for Rowlandson's broker, Ross Taylor, only to be told that he was out of town and wouldn't be back until the next day.

I looked at my watch.

"We've got time to see the banker," he said.

As we went back to the car, I said, "I need to talk to Taylor before I talk to the banker." I picked up Charles Street, and we played the traffic light game again.

"If he was going to run away from home," Magee said, "why didn't he do it a long time ago? It's easy to see there isn't much between them."

"Something must've happened to trigger his flight. Mrs. Rowlandson didn't seem to know anything," I answered.

"Whatever it was, it was a few months ago. He's been planning it for a while."

When we got home, I sent him in through the front door and drove around back. He took the deadbolt off, and I went in the back door. I picked up the mail from the floor and went to the office. A couple of nice checks, overdue. That's good. I could take those guys off the deadbeat list. A couple of bills for me. Two catalogs. And a threatening letter, presumably from Joe Curtis.

"I'LL GET YOU," it said in red ink. Below that was a crude outline of a gun. I must have made a noise, because Magee came running in.

"What?"

I pointed to the letter. He started to pick it up.

"Fingerprints," I said.

I went to the kitchen for a plastic bag to put the letter in.

"I've got to go home and get some stuff," he said as he watched me shove the letter in the bag with my finger.

"I do have a washing machine," I said.

"Just stuff," he said. He went to the back door and stopped. "Throw the deadbolt behind me. I'll be back before dark."

I went to the office to try to get some work done, but the letter had unsettled me, and the drawn curtains seemed to make the walls move in toward me. Diva came and jumped on my lap, and I scratched her ears and ran my hand down her long back. The room was dark and felt forbidding. Stroking the cat helped some, but nothing was going to make me feel better until I got Joe Curtis. I put Diva on the floor, and she followed me to the kitchen, complaining. She twirled around my ankles in an attempt to trip me, her patented way to point out that her food bowl was empty, which it was. I gave her some kibble, and she sat and stared at me.

"You know you don't get wet cat food this time of the day," I said.

She disagreed with me in sharp Siamese, but I ignored her and looked in the freezer for some chicken to fix for dinner. After a few more comments, she deigned to eat some kibble.

I went upstairs into the light to think. I lay down on the bed and stared at the ceiling, which was a mistake, because I fell asleep. When I woke up, it was dark, and Magee wasn't back. I went back downstairs to the office and dialed his number. I let it ring for twenty times and then hung up. He should be back, shouldn't he? He said he be back by dark. I should go and see. Maybe he was in trouble. Maybe he had a blonde again. Maybe that was what he needed to go back for. But he said he'd be back by dark, and he wasn't back. I called again, still no answer. Was it better for me to be embarrassed again or not go when he needed me? *Damned man.* I put the chicken in the refrigerator and put on my coat. There was no way I could engage the deadbolt on the back door. I headed for the beltway and I-70, tapping my fingers on the steering wheel and fretting. The muscles in my neck began to twist. What if it was a blonde? What if it wasn't? I turned off at Route 32 and turned west on Route 144. It hadn't seemed that far last time. When

I turned into his driveway, I saw the Jeep, but the house was dark. Because of the blonde? Why did I keep asking that? It's not as if I had any right to. I got the Maglite out of the glove compartment and turned it on. The snow was dirty, and it looked like I had been the only person to go in the front door. Only one set of tracks. I went up the steps again and pounded on the door. I pounded again. Did I hear something? The front door was unlocked, and I threw it open.

"Magee!" I yelled. "Magee!"

I heard a groan and threw the light in that direction. Magee was laying on the floor curled up in a fetal position.

I reached around the wall to find the light switch and turned it on.

"Anybody else here?"

"No." It was a gasp.

I went to the kitchen; the back door was unlocked. I went back into the living room.

"Keys," I said.

He moved a little and said, "Pocket."

I pushed my fingers into his jeans pocket and pulled a bunch of keys out. I handed them to him.

"Front door."

He handed me a key, and I locked the door. I went back and gave him the keys again.

"Back door."

He handed me a key, and I locked the back door. I put the keys in my pocket and knelt down beside him. He was sweating. I went into the bathroom, got a cold cloth, and wiped his face and hands. I went

138

upstairs to get a pillow and blanket and saw that the room had been searched. I went downstairs, wrapped him up and turned up the space heater.

"The place has been searched."

"Yeah."

"What were they looking for?"

"They didn't say."

"Look, I'm sorry I didn't get here sooner but—"

He grunted. "You were afraid I had a blonde here."

I blushed. "I was afraid you had a blonde here. What happened?"

"Three black guys just kicked the shit out of me."

"Any identifying marks?"

"Would you believe ski masks?"

"I would. Anything else?"

"They kept saying 'where is it?'"

"What? Where is what? What were they looking for?"

His voice was getting stronger. "Look, I was trying to keep my head from getting kicked in."

"There must be something."

He thought. "One of them had a ring. A ring like a skull."

"That ought to be in the thugs file at Fayette Street. Do you mind if I get into your medicine cabinet?"

"What for?"

"Painkiller and maybe some Arnica or Bengay."

"Okay."

I came back with some Extra Strength Tylenol and a tube of Bengay and a glass of water. I pried his body up off the floor, and he hissed in pain. I gave him three Extra Strength Tylenol. I let him down and unbuttoned his shirt. I felt along his ribs, and he hissed again.

"Cold hands."

I went back to the bathroom and ran some warm water over my hands and returned. I gently rubbed some Bengay along his ribs.

"Nothing seems broken, but what do I know?"

"I don't think anything's broken, but a couple of them are cracked."

I sat back on my heels. "You can't sleep on the floor, and I don't think you can sleep on the sofa either." It was a Duncan Phyfe and too short by about a foot. "There must be some way to get you upstairs."

He looked desperate.

"Can you get up on your hands and knees?"

I took the blanket off of him and helped him. By the way he was gritting his teeth, it smarted some. The stairs to the second floor were narrow and didn't have a banister. I stood on the outside so he wouldn't fall off as he climbed one step at a time, slowly. He made it upstairs and crawled over to the bed. I took him under the arms and helped him get up and roll onto the bed. He closed his eyes, panting. I took his boots off and went downstairs. I returned with the pillow, the blanket, and an empty mayonnaise jar. I tucked him in. It would be better to get him out of those jeans; he was going to have seams down his thighs tomorrow, but I quailed at the effort it would take to get them off of him. He looked at the mayonnaise jar in my hand.

"What's that for?"

"In case you have to pee," I replied.

CHAPTER 14

He looked startled.

"Well, do you want to crawl downstairs if you have to go? I'm leaving the light on so I can see you if I come up."

I slept on the couch with my coat over me, and it was too short for me too. I went upstairs a couple of times to check on him; he wasn't running any temperature. The next morning, he looked a little more limber. I rubbed Bengay on his ribs again, helped him out of bed, and put his shoes on for him. He looked irritated.

"You want to bend over and do it yourself?" I asked.

He shook his head no and let me help him stand up and walk to the stairs. He went down the steps with his back against the wall. When he got to the first floor, he stood there panting. Since the mayonnaise jar was empty, I gave him my shoulder to get into the bathroom.

"Going to help me?" he growled.

I grinned at him. "Not unless you want me to."

I heard the toilet flush and an electric razor start up, followed by a groan and the razor shutting down. I went to the kitchen and opened the refrigerator door. Typical bachelor's refrigerator. Four bottles of beer and a loaf of moldy bread. He came out of the bathroom and sat down on the sofa.

"I've got to get some food. How fast can you turn sideways?"

I saw him try to turn to the left and wince.

"If I leave you and they come back, you're dead meat."

He growled again. He was feeling better.

"You're coming with me."

He growled but submitted to my helping him with his coat. We went out the back door, past his Jeep, and down to my car.

"I hate to leave your Jeep exposed, but you're not fit to drive." He frowned mightily but let me help him into the passenger seat and buckle his seatbelt.

"Which do you prefer, Hopkins or Bon Secours?"

"I don't need to go to the hospital," he said with a mulish look on his face.

"You're getting those ribs x-rayed before I take you home."

He continued to look mulish, and I drove to Bon Secours. I have a thing about Hopkins. At the emergency entrance he took exception to being put in a wheelchair.

"Look, Charlie, you're going in a wheelchair if I have to get an orderly. You're an EMT. You know the drill."

"Don't call me Charlie."

I took him to the desk, demanded his insurance card, and checked him in. While they were dealing with him, thank God, I went and moved the car. I went into his cubicle and sat. The look on his face as he lay in a hospital gown was worth the price of admission. Eventually, somebody came.

"Three guys kicked him in the ribs, yesterday," I said. "He needs an x-ray."

The doctor agreed. I went to the waiting room and stared at the walls. Eventually, a nurse called me back to where Magee was sitting in a wheelchair.

"Nothing broken," she said.

He glared.

"Your face will freeze that way," I said and took him out to the car. We got to the front door of my house before I said, "They took the revolver, didn't they?"

"Yeah."

I drove around to the alley and parked in the yard. The back door had been unlocked overnight. I got out of the car and took out my gun. "You stay here," I said.

He didn't. We started through the house. What he thought he could do in his condition, I couldn't think. Diva started weaving her way around my legs to indicate her empty food dish, but I ignored her and went on checking the house. The house was empty, but I found another note from Joe Curtis, this time on my desk.

"I WILL GET YOU" it said in red magic marker.

"I suppose he got tired of waiting," Magee said.

I crumpled the note up and threw it in the wastebasket. He got it back out and put it in the plastic bag with the first note.

"You have a choice between the couch in here and the fireplace or the couch in the living room and the television set."

He sat down on the office couch. I got a pillow and a cover from upstairs and tucked him in again. He scowled.

I turned the gas logs on and sat in my armchair. "Why now?"

Magee grunted. It sounded like a question.

"Why did they search your place and beat you up now?"

"Because that was the first time they could get me alone?" He sounded as if he hurt.

"Maybe. There's a long list of things about your case we don't know. What was Artie Ho doing in Baltimore? Something to do with drugs, probably. What was he doing in that loft building? Who killed him? Where does that Phillips guy fit in? Why did the attacks on you stop after Ho was identified until yesterday?"

Magee hissed in pain as he turned his back on me.

The rest of the day was painful in the extreme.

Harold called after breakfast.

"We need to meet. There's a bar called Sam's on the corner."

"Twenty minutes," I said.

I lifted my coat from the hook beside the back door.

"Where are you going?" he asked.

I put on my gun and holster and replied, "Out."

He got up carefully from the kitchen table. "I'm going with you."

I suppose I could have tied him to a chair.

Sam's Place was one of those corner bars you find all over town. Harold was waiting for us in the back booth. Magee and I sat with our backs to the wall. Magee ordered a beer, and I ordered a Coke.

"The phone's in the hall. I couldn't talk. Phillips went out last night, and he got away before I could get to my car to follow him. Left about eight-thirty, back by ten. I hadn't checked the mileage on the rental. I did after he got back. The room doors have good Yale locks. There's no way I can get into his room. I'm not sure what else I can do."

I heard the door open and looked up to see Phillips look at me and turn away quickly. I was burned, and possibly Harold was too, if Phillips had heard him on the phone and followed him. I told the guys what had happened.

"Check out and put the airline ticket back in Artie Ho's room, then go on home," I told Harold. "I don't have anything for you to do right now, but I may have later."

We sat in the car while I thought about my next move. I put the car in gear and headed toward police headquarters at Fayette Street. Maybe there was another way to get the information I needed. As luck would have it, Homer Kruger was in his office and willing to see us. I took the chair across from his desk, and Magee leaned up against the doorframe with his arms crossed.

Homer mashed his cigarette out in the ashtray and lit another.

"What do you want, Annie? I'm busy."

"I've got some information I think you need, and I know you've got some information I need. Let's trade."

"Why don't I just put you in a room and sweat you?" He stuck his jaw out.

"Don't be that way, Homer. You don't even know what I want to know," I said. "And you don't know what I have to trade."

He chewed on his cigarette for a minute. "Okay. What do you want to know?"

"Did they find heroin on Artie Ho's body at the morgue?"

He looked startled. "Where'd you hear that?"

"I didn't. It's sort of a conclusion. Did they?"

"Yeah, they did. And you're not telling anybody."

"Nope. What kind? From the Golden Triangle?"

"Somebody there is going to get his ass burned."

"Don't bother looking for a leak. There isn't one. Next: did you find any useful prints at the crime scene? There was fingerprint powder all over the place, but it looked like the window frame and the doorknob had been wiped."

"They had."

"The banister?"

"Don't teach your grandmother to suck eggs, Annie."

I grinned at him. "But the Chinese carryout boxes had Artie Ho's prints, right?"

Kruger grunted.

"Now it's my turn. Artie Ho worked for the CIA in Laos during the Vietnamese war collecting and shipping opium bricks."

"How do you know?"

"Magee."

"I was there," Magee said. "I know."

"Harold's got a contact at Langley. He said Ho was working for a Willard MacIntyre in LA. MacIntyre claims to be importing rattan furniture. The Agency had a tail on him for some reason, but he slipped the leash. And before you ask, Harold's contact wouldn't tell him why they were following him. He was surprised that Ho had turned up dead in Baltimore."

"Anything else?" Kruger asked.

"That's not enough?"

Kruger grunted, and we left.

I drove over to Pennsylvania Avenue and parked in front of Billy's Place.

"You're out of your mind!" Magee said.

"Probably." I pushed my way through the door into a smoky bar with tables and booths occupied by black men. A pool table was at the back. The room got very quiet.

"Tyrone Black?" I asked.

A chunky light-skinned man seated at a table by the pool table said "Yo, mama?"

I walked over to his table, Magee muttering behind me. I took a stance with my legs spread.

"I have some information for you. They found the vial of Southeast Asian heroin Artie Ho had on his body at the morgue. My client doesn't have it. Never had it."

"How do you know?" Black asked.

"A cop told me," I answered. "Your thugs roughed up my client two days ago."

"You got balls, mama," he said, surrounded by those thugs.

I put my hand on my gun, and three of them hoisted guns at me. I pulled mine out and took a firing position. "I may go, but he'll go first."

"Put 'em away, boys. Whatcha want, mama?"

I put my gun down beside my leg. "I came to tell you that my client doesn't have anything to do with the West Coast heroin trade. His only connection with Artie Ho was to pick him up out of the street and try to keep him alive. He's an EMT. That's his job. I don't know what Artie was doing in town, but Magee has nothing to do with it."

"The chinks is trying to move in," Black said.

"The chinks, as you call them, are not that stupid. They haven't got soldiers enough to muscle in on your trade." But another black gang does, I thought. "I talked to Wilson Lee at On Leong the other day.

He doesn't know Artie Ho and doesn't know why he was in town. You people ought to talk to each other. Save a lot of gunplay."

Black cocked his head at me. "You believe him, mama?"

"I do. I repeat. The Chinese wouldn't be that stupid. They've got the West Coast. What do they need with the East Coast?"

He nodded his head.

"That guy over there," I said nodding at the guy with the skull-shaped ring, "took my client's revolver. I want it back."

I heard Magee hiss in back of me. Tyrone Black opened his mouth and roared in laughter.

"Balls, mama. You should work for me." He nodded at the guy. "Give it back to her."

Skull Ring looked at him in amazement. "Wha'?"

"I said give it to her."

Skull Ring frowned, but he pulled the revolver out of his belt and put it on the table.

"Get it, Magee," I told him.

Magee walked over carefully and picked up the revolver.

"We good?" I asked Black.

Black nodded, still laughing.

"Pleasure doing business with you," I said and started backing away. About halfway to the door I turned, and we walked out.

CHAPTER 15

We got in the car, and I pulled away.

"You are insane!"

"If I let thugs like Tyrone Black get the better of me, I won't be able to work in this town," I said.

About three blocks from Billy's Place, I began to tremble. I pulled into a vacant parking place and turned off the engine. I looked straight ahead. I put my head on the steering wheel and went on trembling. I handed the keys to Magee.

"At least I didn't throw up this time. You're going to have to drive," I told him, and we changed places.

When we got home, we followed the usual routine. I told Diva I'd feed her later, and we cleared the house. I'm not sure what I could've done if we'd found Joe Curtis. I turned into my bedroom.

"Feed Diva," I said and shut the door. I crawled into bed and pulled the covers over my head, but the

Browning was digging into my hip. I sat up and took the holster and the gun off and put them on the floor. While I was up, I took my boots off too. I lay back down and pulled the covers up over my head again.

There are times when I think Elizabeth's right.

The next day I went into the office with a cup of coffee. I'm missing something, I thought. I missed that spate of shootings. What else have I missed? I crossed to the shelves and picked up the newspapers back to a week before Artie Ho was killed and settled down to go through the crime news. I have a map of Baltimore glued to a board behind the couch. I pulled it out and started plotting the shootings, one pin for each. I could see the groupings and knew Tyrone Black and Willie Reid's people were killing each other. Probably Black was trying to expand into Willie's territory now that Willie was in jail. I plotted Artie Ho's death on the map and realized there was another death that night, one I'd missed. A guy was found shot in an alley off Hollins Street.

I called Harold. "Need you to check a guy out. One DJohn Baker. Found shot in an alley off Hollins Street the night Artie Ho was killed. Who was he and what was he doing in the neighborhood?"

"I suppose you want it yesterday?"

"The day before would be better."

I settled back to think. Artie Ho was in town to sell somebody that heroin. Not Tyrone Black. The logical people to buy it were Willie Reid's people. The only way they could defend themselves against Tyrone

Black was to grow. They could take over the heroin trade in town with a superior product at a lower price. Even if only temporarily. And by killing everybody who came up against them, which is what it looked like they were doing. A gang war, not machine gun battles in the streets, but picking people off one by one. That way only the police would notice and only after a while.

"Are you sure you can't remember anything about that guy who jumped into the ambulance and killed Artie Ho?" I asked Magee.

He looked up from his book. "His head was shaved, and he had a gold tooth in the upper front. I can't even figure out how tall he was. He was just in, rapped me, pulled the lines out, and beat it."

"A black guy with a shaved head and a gold tooth. That describes half the black men in Baltimore. Did you know there was a guy shot in an alley off Hollins Street the same night Artie Ho was killed?"

"No. Were they the only two killed that night?"

"Yes. Connected?"

He shook his head and went back to reading, and I went back to contemplating the pins on the map. It was almost dinnertime when Harold called.

"Baker normally hangs out around the Blue Anchor."

"He's one of Willie Reid's boys?"

"Yeah. I drove over and had a look at the place. A guy with my skin tone can hardly walk around over there in the daytime without being noticed. I saw one other white guy there. Surprised me a little. It was that Roger Phillips guy. I drove around the block a couple of times, and he was attracting attention. I parked and watched. A couple of guys from the Blue Anchor came out and got him. He was still inside when I had to leave. Anything else?"

"Can you hang around there after dark?" I asked him.

"Not a chance," he answered.

What was Roger Phillips doing around Willie Reid's place?

After dinner, I went for my coat. Magee went for his coat.

"Where are we going?"

"The Blue Anchor."

"Where is that, and who's going to kill us when we get there?"

"Down by the docks, and we're not going in. We're just going to have a look around."

"Yeah. Right."

The Blue Anchor was on the ground floor in the middle of a row of nineteenth-century houses. Beside it were ship's chandlers, other bars, and other operations that involved women standing around on the street. Harold was right. There was a lot of foot traffic. I parked, and we watched as the world went by, nobody paying any attention to us. We had been there about an hour when Roger Phillips walked out of the Blue Anchor.

"I think it's time to find out where he fits in all of this," I said to Magee. "Go get him."

Magee stepped over and tapped Phillips on the shoulder. Phillips looked at him and swung. Magee gave him a series of scientific body blows and then a lovely right cross that took him down. Magee ran back to the car.

"Is he out?" I asked.

"Yes." He was a bit out of breath.

"But still breathing?"

"Yes."

All of a sudden there was nobody on the street. I pulled out of the parking place. I drove to the first pay phone I saw and called 911. I told the dispatcher there was a man down outside of the Blue Anchor and hung up.

"What was that about?" I asked him.

"He may call himself Roger Phillips, but his real name is Willard MacIntyre."

We'd been home for about an hour, sitting in the office with the fire logs on, drinking our favorite beverages and discussing where Willard MacIntyre fit into the scheme of things, when a knock came on the door. I turned on the light, and drawing my gun, opened the door carefully. It was Homer Kruger.

"I'll have a beer," he said, taking off his coat. Magee got him a beer, and he joined us in the office in front of the fire. He looked carefully at Magee's knuckles, which showed a bit of wear.

"To what do we owe the honor?" I asked.

"Reba is working 911 dispatch. She recognized your voice," he said.

"Such is fame," I said.

"So what were you doing down there?"

"That guy who was down? He is Willard MacIntyre, Artie Ho's boss. Homer, I think I know how it came down, but nobody is ever going to be able to prove it."

He took a healthy gulp of his beer. "So tell me."

"Artie Ho was in town to sell heroin to Willie Reid's people. They were planning to use it to take over the trade from Tyrone Black. No matter how you cut it, it's better than the stuff Black gets from New York. DJohn Baker was meeting Ho in that loft building to get a sample and talk about terms. Somehow Tyrone Black found out about it. His men ambushed Baker and hauled him off to that alley and shot him. One of them took his place and threw Ho out the window. All of the rest follows from that."

"How do you figure that?" Homer asked.

"Because it has to be about heroin. Artie was here to sell it to somebody. Not Tyrone. He already has a supplier, and they would take serious offense if he tried to change. Who else is there?"

"You've got no evidence."

"I know. It's just logical. No way to prove it, except for Baker's body in the alley maybe. He wouldn't be on that side of town for fun. Just for profit. MacIntyre came to town when he hadn't heard from Artie. After he found out what happened to Artie, he realized that Magee could ID Artie and eventually him, so MacIntyre started attacking Magee. It's important to note that the attacks all failed. Could a real attacker miss so many times? It's also important to note that the attacks stopped when Ho was identified. By that time nobody was believing Magee about how he died. It didn't matter anyway, if Magee didn't find out about who Ho was. That could rip it all apart."

"He must've known that Ho would be identified by his fingerprints," Kruger said.

"He did, but the prints didn't connect Ho to his CIA activities in Laos during the Vietnamese war. Everybody was blaming Magee for Artie's death. He wanted to keep it that way. No connection with drugs and no connection with him"

"So why did Black's men attack me?" Magee asked.

"Because they found out that Artie was carrying a sample, and they assumed you had it. They didn't know any different until I told them the morgue had it."

Kruger finished his beer. "It hangs together, but you're right, no one will ever be able to prove it. I'll check on MacIntyre and see if there are any warrants out on him. Maybe California will take him off our hands."

"I doubt that there are," I said, "but you might learn something useful if you can get the CIA to tell you why they were following Artie. And that furniture importing outfit is definitely suspicious. You might tip the DEA off. He's probably importing stuff from the Golden Triangle. They might like to know."

After Homer left, we sat looking into the fire and trying to figure out how we could prove the story.

Finally, Magee got up and turned off the fire. I turned off the office lights and followed him into the hall.

"It hangs together all right," I said, "but is it true?"

CHAPTER 16

The next day, I called Alex. Brown and found that Ross Taylor was back and would see us at eleven. West Baltimore Street was as crowded as usual, and I had to scoot under the nose of a bus to get into the right-hand lane to turn onto South Street to get to Alex. Brown again, which caused the driver indigestion.

I asked for Ross Taylor at the receptionist's desk, and she told us to have a seat. It was ten tedious minutes of watching money men coming in and going out, before a slender, not to say scrawny, man in an off-the-rack suit approached us, a sour look on his face. Without offering any courtesies, he led us to a conference room on the first floor and shut the door. He didn't ask us to be seated, so I sat down at the head of the table. He looked annoyed, which made me happy. He took a chair, and Magee leaned against the door.

"I can't tell you anything about Glenn Rowlandson's investments," he said bluntly.

You want blunt? I can do blunt. "I don't need you to tell me anything about his investments. I've got the statements." I took them out of my backpack and put them on the table. Showing him the oldest one, I said, "You'll see his holdings before he started cashing them in." I handed him the most recent one. "You'll see that he's cashed in everything except a minuscule amount to keep the portfolio open. I don't need any information about the account."

His pale blue eyes glittered. He patted his skull to make sure that the strands of hair there were properly in place. "Then what do you want?"

"If I ever have a portfolio, it's not going to live at Alex. Brown," I commented. "Rowlandson has gone missing. His wife hired me to find him, because she thought he was having a blackout, wandering around not knowing who he was. The evidence of his statements, however, suggests that he's been planning to do a flit for some time." I picked up the first statement. "At least six months."

"So you don't need anything from me," he said.

"I need whatever you can tell me. He's gone off and left his wife without a penny, and I need to find him, if only to shake some of that money out of him."

He got up and turned to the door facing Magee; Magee didn't move. He turned back to me. "I have no information for you. I didn't ask him about his plans, and he didn't tell me. I followed his instructions and sold his holdings. Other than that I have no knowledge. Now, if you'll excuse me?"

I wouldn't. "I see no indication here that you were following Colonel Rowlandson's instructions when you sold his investments."

Taylor sputtered. "Of course I was following his instructions!"

"Can you provide Mrs. Rowlandson's attorney with copies of those instructions?"

He sputtered again. "Of course not. He instructed me by telephone."

"I hope you recorded those phone calls, because if you didn't, Mrs. Rowlandson's attorney will be talking to the state's attorney. Rowlandson's money has disappeared, possibly fraudulently."

"Mrs. Rowlandson is not a party to the account."

"She is if he's dead. Where did you put the money?"

He maintained his aggressive stance.

"Fraud," I reminded him.

He thought it over briefly, and his shoulders twitched. "I gave it to him in a series of cashier's checks. I don't know what he did with it after that."

"You're not kidding, are you?"

"I never kid about financial affairs," he snapped.

"And you just let him walk out of here with cashier's checks?" I asked incredulously.

"I advised him against it," he said defensively, "but in the end it was his money. He could do anything he liked with it; I followed his instructions."

Magee moved aside. Taylor opened the door and turned on his heel with no farewell.

We picked up the car. "Have you ever considered a career in diplomacy?" Magee asked.

"I knew when I saw his sour puss that I was not going to get much out of him. It took the threat of legal action to get that much." In my frustration, I ground a gear.

"Simmer down. There's no point in destroying the transmission. It's possible he was telling you the truth. Why should Rowlandson tell him why he was selling out?"

"I can't believe he didn't ask."

"Rowlandson was planning to disappear. Why would he tell anybody where he was going? In fact, it would be a good idea not to. He said he advised against it."

"And now he's in the wind with a series of cashier's checks that anybody can cash."

Since the next stop was the First National Bank of Maryland at Light and Redwood, I took Lombard Street to Light and parked. I don't often get a chance to have a corned beef sandwich at Attman's Delicatessen.

I ordered corned beef on rye.

"What kind of mustard you want?" the waiter asked.

"Brown but not hot," I replied. "And don't forget the kosher pickle."

"You're going to interview a banker with garlic on your breath?" Magee asked.

"Absolutely," I replied. The corned beef was even better than I remembered and so was the kosher pickle.

The First National Bank was not far from the delicatessen as the crow flies, but no crow ever flew across downtown Baltimore. I finally found a parking place, and we climbed over piles of dirty yellowing snow to the bank. The building had not changed on the outside, but the banking room had been modernized since I'd been there last. The marble floors remained, but the brass chandeliers and brass cages at the tellers' stations had disappeared, replaced by dark wood and indirect lighting. We stepped through the gate into the manager's space. The manager, William Stock, had a decorative receptionist, all blond hair and blue eye shadow, and she was typing hard as we approached her desk. How anybody can type with three-inch fingernails has always baffled me. I gave her my card and asked to see Mr. Stock.

"May I tell him why you're calling?"

"It's about one of his clients, Glenn Rowlandson. He's disappeared."

"Disappeared!" She looked startled.

"Disappeared."

She came back quickly and took us into the manager's office. William Stock was a late middle-aged man with a lot of white hair and a white mustache. He tended to corpulence, and his ears stuck out a little. He was wearing hand-tailored tweeds and had the manner of a country gentleman. He settled us in chairs before his mahogany desk.

"Now, what's all this about Glenn Rowlandson being missing?" he asked.

"He's been gone over two weeks, and Mrs. Rowlandson thinks he's had a blackout. She's hired me to find him."

"Nonsense! Glenn Rowlandson never has black-outs."

"I think you're right. I think he's been planning to disappear for some time."

He harrumphed and turned it into a cough. "More nonsense!"

"Mr. Stock, Glenn Rowlandson ran a fair amount of money through his checking account. Do you know where it went?"

"I can't reveal that information to you, Miss Carter."

I showed him the bank statements.

"Mrs. Rowlandson has no right to that information."

"She does if he's dead. And he might well be dead."

"You have no proof of that."

I handed him the last four bank statements, which showed the balance going down to $50,000. It also showed his army pension and Social Security missing. He read through the statements, put them on his desk, and put a paperweight over them.

"These papers prove nothing."

"What happened to his pension and Social Security, Mr. Stock? The government doesn't like its money going astray."

He drummed his fingers on his blotter for a moment and finally called his secretary. "Miss Jensen, please bring me the file of Colonel Glenn Rowlandson." He sat back in his chair to wait. It wasn't long before Miss Jensen brought him the file. He leafed through it and looked up.

"The pension and Social Security were transferred to the account of Mrs. Vivian Rowlandson."

So he left her some money. "And the rest of it?" I prodded.

"It went into cashier's checks."

Glenn Rowlandson was certainly collecting a lot of cashier's checks. "And this $50,000 check drawn to cash?"

Stock looked a little embarrassed. "He cashed it himself."

"And?"

"He cashed it while I was on vacation. I would never have allowed him to do it."

"Do what, Mr. Stock?"

"He took it in hundred-dollar bills and walked out the door."

"I hope that $50,000 in cash didn't contribute to his disappearance," I said.

There was no escaping it. Glenn Rowlandson had been planning to disappear for at least six months. What triggered that flight? And Phi went with him. Where did they go? The police had found the MG at the airport. Did that mean he flew somewhere? Or was it just a convenient place to stash the car? I looked at Magee.

"If you wanted to lose a car, where would you put it?"

He thought. "Not on the ground at the airport. I'd put it deep inside a multistory parking garage. Even a red MG could be unnoticed for a long time."

I nodded. "Me too. You think that means that they flew somewhere?"

"Maybe. It would help if we could find the station wagon."

The first thing I did when we got inside, after clearing the house, was to call Vivian Rowlandson.

"Mrs. Rowlandson, have you checked your bank statement lately?"

"No. There's never anything in the account. Why?"

"Your husband didn't give you an allowance?"

"Yes. Enough for groceries."

"Find your last bank statement, and call me back."

She called me back within ten minutes. "What's this, Miss Carter? These government checks?"

"They're your husband's pension and Social Security. He transferred them to your account before he left."

"He really is gone."

"Both of them are gone. What do you want me to do now?"

She answered after a long pause. "You still have to find him. I'll have no idea when he dies and I inherit the property. Find him, please."

"Mrs. Rowlandson, he's making every effort not to leave a trail. I'm not sure I can find him, but I'll try," I told her.

"He hasn't gone to see any of his friends except Osborne," Magee said.

165

"No. He hasn't, has he? But he was still around as of last week when he visited Osborne."

I thought about that as I went to the kitchen to figure out what to have for dinner. Nothing in the refrigerator looked good. Nothing in the freezer looked good. If I wanted to cook every night, I'd get a husband. Sending out for a pizza sounded like a good idea. Back in the office, Magee had turned on the gas fire logs and was reading Simpson's book about the Green Berets again. He looked up.

"Chinese or pizza? One or the other, unless you want to cook."

"Okay, pizza."

I settled down with Rowlandson's address book. Many of the addresses had been crossed out, and many of them were for people like plumbers. "Magee, Rowlandson didn't seem to have many friends."

He looked up from his book. "Not many in Viet Nam either, in the field or at headquarters. He was a quiet guy."

"What did you think of him?"

"It's hard to say. Whenever he showed up at my vill, he was in the way. You know, what you really want is a major looking over your shoulder."

"Did he do anything to get in the way or was it just his being there?"

He looked into the fire. "You know, he never gave orders, he never countermanded an order. He was just there, looking sad and sick. They should have boarded him long before they did. He was just *there*."

"He had no friends? Nobody he was close to?"

"Nobody but his old sergeant, and even they didn't talk much. It was more like they had an emotional bond of some kind."

I raised my eyebrows.

"No, not like that. Just like some kind of mental connection."

I called a few individuals whose numbers I found. The entries looked old, and a couple of them had trouble remembering who Glenn Rowlandson was. I had the feeling that I had in his room again—that Glenn Rowlandson didn't actually exist.

Magee put the book down hard. I looked up. "This is not going to turn out well."

It hadn't, had it? All those years and all those tears, and we lost.

The pizza came, and we ate it and returned to the office. Magee picked up the Simpson book again. He couldn't stay away from it. I was going through the stack of To Be Read by my chair and seriously considering going into the living room and watching a sitcom when the phone rang.

It was Jack. "Annie! Elizabeth's been kidnapped!"

CHAPTER 17

My heart stopped, and I dropped the phone.

Magee jumped up. "Annie! What's wrong?"

I put my hand to my throat. "It's Joe. Joe Curtis. He's got Elizabeth."

Magee picked up the phone. "What happened, Jack?" he asked and listened to the answer. "We'll be right over."

I was cold. Cold all over. I'd never been so cold before.

"Annie, come on." He shook me.

I stirred, and he shook me again.

"We're going over to Jack's. Come on."

He took me by the hand and pulled me up. Once on my feet, I began to move slowly, blindly. In the kitchen Magee helped me with my coat, and I gave him the keys to my car so he could drive. I stared blindly at the windshield. Joe Curtis had Elizabeth.

I knew what he wanted.

Jack let us into the apartment and began pacing, worried, frightened, almost hysterical. "You!" He pointed at me. "This is *your* fault!"

Magee helped me off with my coat, and I slumped down on the couch. It was my fault. I hugged myself and rocked back and forth. I was cold. So cold.

"Jack," Magee said.

Jack continued pacing and raving. "Elizabeth is involved in one of your filthy cases! And now this murderer has got her!"

Magee grabbed his arm. "Jack. Stop it! This won't help Elizabeth. Tell us."

"I knew something was wrong. Elizabeth was supposed to pick me up at the airport. I called the house, and when nobody answered, I took the shuttle into the Mayflower and took a taxi home. Here. The lights were on; when I came in I found *this.*" He had a crumpled piece of paper in his hand. He waved it at me, and Magee took it from him. We looked at it.

"I'LL GET BACK TO YOU," it said in red magic marker, another of Joe Curtis's patented messages.

Magee pushed Jack into a chair and went to the kitchen. He returned with two bottles of beer. "Where's the gin?"

Jack waved in the direction of the cabinet against the right-hand wall, and Magee got the gin, poured a healthy slug into a glass, and handed it to me. I tossed it off and handed him the class. He refilled it. I sipped that one, and gradually I began to thaw, and my brain began to work.

"Have you called the police?" I asked.

"No," Jack replied.

"Don't," I said. "Has he called?"

Jack took a long pull of the beer. "No."

We sat in silence as a clock on the wall ticked. Magee got up and got more beer and looked to question me. I shook my head no, and we went on sitting.

"Why doesn't he call?" Jack asked desperately.

"He softening us up," I said.

Jack pounded his fist on the arm of his chair. "I'm soft! He needs to tell us what to do!"

"He won't call tonight," Magee said. "We're going home. If he calls, call us."

Jack nodded.

In the car I said, "I know what he wants. He wants me."

My girl, who hated my job, was in the hands of the man who killed her father. I rubbed my face. I should cry, shouldn't I? I pounded my fists on the dashboard. "I should do something. I need to do something," I told Magee.

"Yes."

"What?"

"Wait."

There was no need to clear the house. Joe Curtis wasn't there. I put some cat food down and went upstairs, closing the door. I sat in the chair and looked out the window, the blue Princess phone beside me on the bed.

I didn't sleep. At six o'clock I decided to get up. I went downstairs and made coffee, poured a cup, and went to the office. Magee came in just as I opened the curtains.

"I figure he's not going to shoot the place up today," I said and sat at the desk. I went on sitting and drinking coffee until the pot was empty. I washed it out and made another pot.

I poured another cup of coffee and continued waiting. The day passed, minute by minute, and nothing happened. Magee got some chicken soup out of the freezer and thawed it. After a while he brought a bowl and spoon into the office and put it on the desk in front of me.

"Eat it," he commanded. "You've got to eat something."

I picked up the spoon and ate some until my stomach rebelled. I put the spoon down and went upstairs to my bedroom and shut the door. I sat on the chair in front of the window as before. I looked out the window as before. I didn't sleep as before. I knew I had to get some sleep if I was to do something about Joe Curtis, so I lay on the bed, and, against all the odds, I fell asleep. I woke when the first light came through the window and resumed sitting and watching and waiting.

At eight, Jack called. "When is he going to call?" He sounded more desperate.

"When he's ready," I replied. He slammed down the receiver.

Downstairs, Magee was drinking coffee and looking at the sports page. "He'll call today," he said.

"Maybe."

171

"It's hard to keep somebody prisoner. He'll call today."

"Maybe she's dead," I said.

"He'd call to tell you that."

Cheerful thought.

At five-thirty Jack called. "He called. He's going to call back."

"Did he say what he wants?" I asked.

"No. He said he'd call back."

"Did you ask to speak with her?" I asked.

"What?"

"Did you ask to talk to her?"

"No. Why should I?"

"To make sure she's alive," I said.

"Annie!"

"Just do it! We're on our way."

Magee and I walked to the back door. When we got there, I stopped and turned back. "You go on. There are a couple of things I have to do. I'll be there in a few minutes."

Magee looked at me skeptically. "Go. Go," I said.

He shrugged his shoulders and went. I went back to the office and waited. After five minutes, the phone rang. It was Joe Curtis.

My throat was almost too tight to talk, but I managed.

"What do you want?"

"Why, Annie, I want you."

"Where are you? I'll come."

"You know Dickeyville?"

"Yes."

"Wetheredsville Road?"

"Yes."

"Take Wetheredsville Road from Dickeyville through Leakin Park toward town. On the left there's a bridge over the Gwynns Falls that leads to a bunch of craft shops. Take it. You'll find us in the largest building. And Annie, you call the cops, she's dead."

"I know. I'll be there."

There wasn't any point in taking a gun, but I made what preparations I could. I left a note on my desk.

"If I'm not here when you get back, go to Dickeyville and take Wetheredsville Road through Leakin Park toward town." I gave him the rest of the directions, but if we weren't back by the time he figured it out and came back, we'd both be dead.

Very large butterflies occupied my stomach. I used every calming mechanism I knew, and by the time I got to the bridge over the Gwynns Falls I thought I could do it. I had to do it. The first building was a large cinderblock structure. There were lights on. I parked and pushed the door open. The building was empty except for two chairs and two people over near the far wall: Elizabeth and Joe Curtis. Elizabeth, her face tear-stained, sat slumped on a chair, unbound. Joe Curtis sat in the other chair, teetering back on two legs against the wall, a gun on her. She ran to me and I put my arms around her.

"Ain't that sweet?" Curtis sneered.

"If we're going to get out of this alive, I need you to be strong," I whispered to her. "When we get home we can have hysterics together."

"Now, now. No secrets." He stood up.

"It's me you want," I said. "Let her go."

He roared with laughter. "I'm going to do both of you, her first. Maybe I'll play with her little first."

I felt Elizabeth tremble. I went down on one knee and flipped my left pant leg up, ripping out the knife taped to my ankle. I rushed at him as hard as I could, ramming him up against the wall, sticking the point of the knife under his chin. I felt blood. Good.

"Drop the gun, Joe, unless you want me to slit your throat." I pushed the knife farther into his chin. "Drop the gun."

He dropped it.

"Elizabeth, get the gun!"

She got the gun.

"Now come around behind me and give it to me in my right hand." She did, and I threw the knife away and backed away from Curtis. "Now go to one of the shops and break a window. That should start a burglar alarm, but try to go inside and call 911." I turned to Joe Curtis. "Sit down on the floor and put your hands on your head." He didn't move. "Move! Just give me a reason to kill you." I sounded mean. I felt mean. He sat down, and I sat on the chair Elizabeth had been sitting in. Soon I heard a burglar alarm and a siren. I heard a car scratch in and a door slam. A cop stood in the doorway, gun drawn.

"Gun," I said and put it on the floor.

He stepped inside and kicked the gun away. "Now what's all this?"

I heard another siren and another car and another slammed door and saw another cop with his gun drawn.

I pointed at Joe Curtis with my chin. "This is Joe Curtis. He's wanted for two murders. He kidnapped my daughter."

"Why is he bleeding?" the first cop asked.

"Because I stabbed him." I pointed to the knife on the floor.

Elizabeth returned. "He was going to kill us."

The next car held a plainclothes detective. "What's going on?" he asked.

"This woman says this guy is wanted for two murders, and he kidnapped her daughter."

The detective came and stood over me. "Identification?" He put his hand out.

"I'm a licensed private investigator," I said. "My ID is in my wallet in my left hip pocket."

"Get it."

I got my wallet out and gave him my driver's license and PI license. "Homer Kruger at Fayette Street knows all about this. Perhaps you should call him?"

I could see that he didn't want to call the head of the homicide squad and get him out of bed, but he did.

Another car drove up and slammed its brakes on. Magee and Jack bolted through the door and stopped.

"Who are you?" the detective asked.

Jack ran to Elizabeth and took her in his arms.

"Jack Winslow," I said. "Elizabeth's boyfriend."

Magee crossed to me and draped his arm over my shoulder.

"My name's Magee. I'm her client." He looked at me. "Did you have to do this by yourself?"

"Yes, I did."

Elizabeth turned in Jack's arms. "Mama, I knew you'd come."

"Of course," I replied.

The next car to arrive belonged to Homer Kruger. It looked like he'd dressed in a hurry. The cuffs of his pajama bottoms were peeping out from under his slacks.

"I take it this is Joe Curtis."

"Yes. He kidnapped Elizabeth. He knew I'd come."

"Why is he bleeding?"

"I knifed him," I said and pointed to the small serrated knife on the floor.

He went over and picked it up and looked at it curiously. "What is it?"

"A tomato slicing knife," I answered. "Homer, can we go home? You can tell them about it."

"First, tell me what happened here."

"He kidnapped Elizabeth. He called me and told me where to come, and I came. He said he was going to kill both of us, so I ran him against the wall and stuck the knife under his chin and told him to drop the gun. He dropped the gun. Elizabeth went to call 911. People started coming." I leaned against Magee, and he propped me up.

"Kruger, she's had it," he said.

"Elizabeth has too," Jack said.

Kruger nodded. "Take them home. They can make statements tomorrow."

I gave my keys to Magee. "You drive." Jack and Elizabeth got into his car.

We drove down Wetheredsville Road toward the city. I leaned my head against the back of the seat.

"You good?" Magee asked.

"I guess. I never hurt anybody before, but I wanted to kill him so bad. I feel all hollow inside."

"That's the way it feels," he said.

CHAPTER 18

When we got home, Diva conned some wet cat food out of me because my brain was too scrambled to remember that she had already had some. I poured myself some gin and went to the office and turned on the gas logs. I'd almost gotten Elizabeth killed. I sat in the chair and stared into the fire. Why was I a private detective anyway? Why wasn't I a secretary or something? After the divorce, Milton could give me only about fifty dollars a month for child support, so I had to get a job, but the jobs I was qualified for wouldn't pay me enough for the two of us to survive. I found an ad from the Pinkerton Agency for trainee detectives, and I followed it up. The trainee salary was more than that for the average secretary, so I went and interviewed, visions of Sam Spade dancing in my head, and they hired me. The Pinkerton Agency is a huge outfit and does all sorts of work. Security was the largest part of what they did in Baltimore, but they liked big beefy guys for that. I got some personal security jobs, but not many, because I couldn't work 24/7. I didn't have anybody to take care of Elizabeth. I thought I was going to get fired over that. Divorce work tended to be nighttime work too, and I was glad I didn't get any of that. I proved to be very good at business crime—fraud, embezzlement, and selling company secrets. After working for the Pinks for a couple of years, I decided I didn't really like the agency. It was too big, too bureaucratic, and after I saved some money, I went out on my own, taking some clients with me. It was a near thing financially for a while, but my clients spread the word, and I began making enough money to survive.

Elizabeth had always hated my job. It wasn't ladylike enough to suit her, but I'd never been girly. She just never noticed it when I was staying home baking cookies.

And now I'd almost gotten her killed.

Magee was sitting on the sofa. I looked at him.

"What if I'd failed?"

"But you didn't."

I had trouble getting over that. Every time I closed my eyes, I watched Joe Curtis shoot Elizabeth. I didn't wake up screaming. I don't scream. I just couldn't wake up, and it happened over and over again.

I told Magee he didn't have to protect me anymore, but he stuck around, watching sports on TV and eating me out of house and home.

At the end of the week, Vivian Rowlandson got me up at six o'clock to yell at me.

"When the hell are you going to find my husband?" she demanded. "I haven't heard from you in a week. What are you doing? I've got his pension and Social Security now, but it's not enough to live on. I've got to hire a stable boy."

Well, sell the damned horses. That'll give you some money to live on, I thought but didn't say. "I just finished a very delicate operation," I said.

"You're supposed to be working for me!"

"You didn't buy my exclusive time," I said. "I told you, there's not much more I can do for you. Your husband disappeared deliberately, and he covered his tracks well."

"There must be something you can do."

I sighed. "All right, I'll see what I can do."

I got out the materials on the Rowlandson case and went over them again. I called the two or three names in the address book I hadn't called before. They hadn't seen him and wanted to know why I was calling. I explained that he was missing, but that didn't help. They hadn't seen him in years. All I had left was his doctor's number and a number with 66 before it and no identification. I made an appointment for the next day to see his doctor, Eugene Potter, at the VA hospital downtown, and had closed down for the day when Elizabeth and Jack showed up bearing food.

Elizabeth had dark circles under her eyes. She kissed me on the cheek and sat down to look at the fire. Coming close to being killed had made her pensive.

Jack, however, was pumped. He couldn't sit down or stay in one place. He paced and waved his arms.

"Annie, you nearly got her killed!"

Elizabeth looked up from the fire. "But she didn't," said Elizabeth. "She came and got me."

"She wouldn't have had to if she hadn't pissed off Joe Curtis."

"Jack! He killed my *father*!"

"He wouldn't have done that if she hadn't stuck her nose in his business."

I wasn't sure how I could answer that. He had been my client.

Elizabeth went back to looking at the fire.

Jack said, "It'll happen again! There's no way I can keep you safe."

She looked back up. "Not if you're out of the country half of the time."

"Elizabeth, it's my job," he said.

"Well, detecting is her job."

Magee took Jack by the shoulder and pointed him to the door. "Let's go see what's for dinner," he said.

"He's right. It might happen again," I said from the chair behind the desk. "Things happen sometimes, but I've never had anyone attack me in my own home before. It might happen again."

"I know it might, Mama. And Jack might get killed in some hellhole he's photographing." She ran her hands through her hair and twisted a lock around her finger. "And I could get run over crossing the street."

"Ah. You've learned that life is unpredictable."

"Yes," she said.

"And every new day is a gift."

She smiled shakily. "Now teach Jack that."

"He already knows it," I said. "He just expects you to be safe."

"When any day a piano might fall on my head as I come out of the office?" she said and smiled.

I smiled back. "What's for dinner?"

"The usual. Steak and salad."

"I think it's safe to let them fix dinner."

"This probably means we'll have to wash the dishes."

"Only the ones that won't go in the dishwasher."

There was no pacifying Jack. He had been too frightened. All Magee and I could do ourselves was to hope and count the odds that it wouldn't happen again.

The Veterans Administration hospital down on Green Street was an impressive brick pile, and if we didn't stop having wars, it was going to have to be enlarged. The outside of the building looked modern. Inside, the place looked old and army—scuffed green walls, GSA furniture, asbestos tile floors. The appropriation was being spent on the patients, not on interior decoration. The receptionist was a late middle-aged woman with white hair piled on top of her head, wearing a navy blue polyester pants suit. The only touch of color in the room was a red plastic rose in a vase on her desk. She raised the telephone receiver and dialed two numbers.

"Go right in," she said and pointed to a door to the left.

Eugene Potter was a chubby man with sandy hair cut short, yellowing teeth, and fingers stained with nicotine. The ashtray on his desk was overflowing, and there was a cigarette burning in his fingers. He wore a white coat with his name embroidered on the chest and looked at the world through thick glasses. There were files scattered on his desk, and both inbox and outbox were full of other files. He rose to shake our hands.

"Sorry about the mess," he said. "Nobody ever has time to file."

"As I told you on the phone, doctor," I said, "Glenn Rowlandson has disappeared. His wife thought at first that he was having a blackout, and she hired me to find him. Colleagues say he's never been known to black out, and I found evidence to suggest that he's been planning to disappear for some time."

The doctor looked concerned. "What evidence?"

"Have you treated Colonel Rowlandson before?"

"What evidence?" he repeated.

"Dr. Potter, are you a psychologist? Or do you specialize in some other form of mental disorder?"

"If you'd looked me up, you wouldn't have had any trouble discovering that I specialize in tropical medicine. And yes, I've treated Glenn Rowlandson before, once when he was in the hospital in Japan and once at Walter Reed. Now what evidence do you have that he was planning to disappear?"

I looked at Magee and back at Potter. "He's been cashing in his investments."

"When did this start?"

"About six months ago."

The doctor leaned back in his chair and took his glasses off. He chewed on an earpiece while deciding how much to tell me. "You realize that I can tell you little about Glenn's condition. Doctor-patient confidentiality."

"Dr. Potter, there's something very wrong going on. About six months ago, Glenn Rowlandson began to sell his investments. He disappeared three weeks ago, leaving his wife with very little money, just his pension and Social Security, to run a large country estate. I need to find him and shake out some money for her. Now tell me what's going on."

"He didn't tell his wife?"

"He didn't tell his wife anything. You are not his family doctor, I assume. Why did he come to you?"

"No, I'm not his regular doctor." He made up his mind and leaned forward with his elbows on his desk. "Glenn came to me because he thought the combination of conditions he acquired in Southeast Asia had returned. Dengue fever. He was riddled with parasites. I would get him reasonably well, and he'd go back to the field. Nobody could keep him out of the field."

"I know that. Everybody says the same thing. He was obsessed with fieldwork in Viet Nam."

Magee shifted in his chair. "Not Viet Nam. Laos."

"Okay. Not Viet Nam."

"I did some tests. He still had a bunch of parasites, but that wasn't what was causing the problem. The problem was that he has pancreatic cancer."

I was shocked. "There's no treatment, is there?" I asked.

"Chemotherapy, but essentially no, there's no treatment. Diagnosis is a death sentence," he replied.

"How long?" I asked.

"Six months to a year," Potter said.

There wasn't much more to say. Magee and I shook hands with Potter and left.

As we drove back to Twenty-Fifth Street, Magee said, "He bought gold."

I looked at him and nearly rear-ended the guy in front of me who was stopped for a traffic light.

"He was diagnosed six months ago. That time is crucial. He's going somewhere where he can't use the US dollar."

"Like Laos?"

"Like Laos."

"But he can't do that. Laos is closed. They kill people who try to get in."

"What's he got to lose?"

When I got home, I avoided the starving cat and went to the office. Magee followed me.

"Let me see that address book," he said.

I handed it to him and he flipped through to the last page.

"This 66 number. It's just jotted in, and it's crooked. It looks more recent than the one above it. Sixty-six is an international code. Give me the telephone book."

After looking at the international numbers, he reached the phone and I got up to let him have the chair. After a few minutes I heard him speak.

"Fred? This is Charlie Magee. Yeah, long time. Listen, have you seen Glenn Rowlandson recently? Ten days ago? What did he want? And you sent him? Where?"

Magee looked at me and shook his head. He listened for a long time.

"Ban Ban Tho? He would have gone anyway with or without a guide? How did he look? Pale. Yeah. Listen, I've got to go. I'll get back to you."

"What?" I asked.

"That was the Paris Bar in Bangkok. All the guys used to hang out there during the war in Laos—Air America crews, CIA guys, some of us. Rowlandson was there ten days ago. Wanted Fred to get him a guide to take him into Laos. Fred tried to talk him out of it, but he was determined to go. Fred got him a Hmong, a guy from one of the refugee camps who he knows goes over into Laos fairly often."

"What's Ban Ban Tho?"

"A vill about five miles from Khe Sanh, about fifty miles from the Mekong River."

"But that's insane! Surely that's a two-day march for a healthy man."

"Probably more on a jungle trail."

"They can't possibly go for two days without being picked up by a government patrol."

"Rowlandson used to be pretty good."

"But he's dying."

I took back my chair. Glenn Rowlandson had been obsessed with getting into the field in Viet Nam. Or was he obsessed with getting into Laos? Did he have a woman there? "Magee, what did Rowlandson do when he joined you in the field? Did he go along with you on patrol, or did he slip away?"

"You mean did he slip off to one of the vills?"

"Yes, did he slip away to one of the vills? Did he have a woman there? A family?"

"I don't know. Maybe he did. He wasn't with my bunch all the time." Magee rubbed his chin. "What now?"

A very good question. Vivian Rowlandson was a pain in the neck, but she deserved better than she had gotten from the men in her life.

"If he dies in Laos," Magee said, "Mrs. Rowlandson will never find out."

"And it'll be seven years before she can have him declared legally dead," I added.

I tended to the mail and found a couple of checks, which I went out and deposited. My balance was looking pretty good for a change. Maybe it was time to take that vacation. Back in the office, I got some travel brochures from the bottom drawer of my desk and sat in my armchair reading them. Bermuda? Jamaica? The Yucatán? I've always wanted to see the Mayan ruins.

"That's all you're going to do?" asked Magee. "Go on vacation?"

"Look, Magee, why don't you go home? Your case is over, and you're safe. My case is over, and I'm safe.

You don't need to protect me, and I don't need to protect you. Go home."

"The Rowlandson case is not over, and you know it."

The rest of the day we sat in the office, glaring at each other when our eyes met. Magee fixed dinner, what he was good at—a pair of steaks and salad. We glared at each other across the table, and I put the dishes in the dishwasher and went back to the office to study my vacation brochures. We watched the eleven o'clock news and stomped our various ways upstairs to bed. Sleep wouldn't come to me, and I tossed and turned.

I did know the Rowlandson case wasn't over, but what could I do?

The next day we went out to The Gables to talk to Vivian Rowlandson. She didn't take the news well.

"Glenn's gone to Laos!" she screamed. "*Now* what am I supposed to do? Okay, he's dying. As far as I'm concerned, he never was alive. He's going to die over there, and I'll never be able to sell this damned place and get away from it!"

I'd thought about that all night, and I'd finally thought of something that might work.

"You need to talk to Mr. Withers."

"Who's he?" Vivian demanded.

"Archibald Withers, your husband's attorney. I'm thinking he can draft a document turning the property over to you. It would have to be signed and witnessed, but I think he could do it."

"And how are we supposed to get it to him in Laos?"

"I don't know, Vivian. First we have to find out if it can be done."

I went upstairs to Rowlandson's study and called Withers. It took a lot of convincing. Who was going to witness such a document that a Maryland court would accept? How are we going to get the document to Rowlandson?

"One thing at a time," I said. "Can you draw up a document?"

Withers cleared his throat, and there was silence on the line. It was taking him a long time.

"Mr. Withers? Can you do it?"

He cleared his throat again. "It would be a violation of Mr. Archer's expressed intentions."

"I doubt that Mr. Archer foresaw the current situation. His intention was to punish Vivian for her mother's behavior. Did he intend to leave her penniless?"

"She must have some money."

"Yes, Glenn transferred his army pension and Social Security to her account before he left. That's not enough to keep a twenty-five-acre estate and ten horses going."

"She could sell some horses."

"Yes, she could, and I'm going to recommend it. Now will you draft the document?"

"Yes. I see that Glenn's dying in Laos would be impossible to prove. I'll have it ready by ten o'clock tomorrow."

I went downstairs and told Vivian what I had asked Withers to do and gave her directions to his office. On the way back to the house, Magee said, "This isn't going to end well."

Because I charged him with eating me out of house and home, Magee went out and got some groceries. We had chicken for dinner. Magee is a better cook than I am.

We met Vivian Rowlandson at Withers's office the next morning. Withers offered his hand to Vivian.

"It's been a long time," he said.

She touched his hand with two fingers. "Since my father died," she said and took a chair.

Withers cleared his throat and waved Magee and me to chairs.

"I've drawn up the document Miss Carter requested," he said, handing us each copies.

I read mine. He must be a pretty good lawyer, because the simple request to transfer the ownership of The Gables to Vivian was tied up in ribbons of legalese and finished with a bow.

"It looks like it should do," I said. "Vivian? What do you think?"

"If you say so, I'll take your word for it." She threw her copy on Withers's desk.

"There is one stipulation," Withers said.

"There would be, of course," I said. "What?"

"This document requires the signatures of two witnesses. The only witnesses I will find acceptable are you, Miss Carter, and your colleague."

I stared at him. "There's not enough money in the world."

I walked to the window and stood with my hands on my hips, staring down into Reed Street, but it wasn't the traffic I saw. I saw myself stuck in a hope-less marriage, Elizabeth just a baby. I saw Daisy Archer, looking for love in all the wrong places. And I saw poor Ethel Curtis, dead at the hands of her brutal husband. Why can't women learn to take care of themselves?

I turned to look at Vivian Rowlandson. Tears were streaming down her cheeks, making streaks in her orange rouge. Dammit, why do I feel responsible for a woman I don't even like?

I looked at Magee. He shrugged one shoulder, re-fusing the decision. I went back to stand in front of Withers's desk. Did he know what he was asking of me? Perhaps he did, but still he asked. Laos is closed and has a vicious communist government. I looked back at Vivian.

"Please, Miss Carter—Annie," she begged.

Her silly clown face broke my heart. There was no way out.

"All right, I'll go, but you're going to have to give me some money. As it stands now there's no way you can pay my bill. I'm not going to charge two tickets to Bangkok on my credit card."

"But I don't have any money."

"Sell a horse," I said. "Quickly. We may be able to catch him before he gets very far."

Withers looked at me. "I'll pay for the tickets and the hotel," he said. "She'll have money soon."

"And the rest?"

"And the rest," he agreed.

As we drove into the traffic on Reed Street, Magee repeated, "This won't end well."

CHAPTER 19

Bangkok - Laos

I stepped out of the Bangkok airport terminal and got slammed in the face with a hot wet towel. I gasped. I was instantly soaked down to and including my underwear.

Magee grinned. "Welcome to Southeast Asia," he said.

The next thing I noticed was the noise, followed by the exhaust fumes. Bangkok had cars and buses and motorcycles and little Jeep taxis, and all of them were honking and spewing fumes. Magee got us a taxi, and we joined the traffic jam. Or maybe it was a parking lot. Hundreds of cars, buses, and bikes moved along at a glacial pace, filling the night with noxious fumes. Eventually, we got to Patpong and drove along looking at the night sights.

"Bangkok invented neon," he said.

"And sex too," I said, reading what the neon said.

It made the neon signs advertising striptease in the Block look trivial in comparison.

"I forgot how raunchy it is," he said.

"Maybe the last time you saw it, you were not in the company of a gently reared lady."

He snorted.

The Paris Bar was fairly small, all smooth, mellow wood, a bar with stools and hundreds of bottles of whiskey against the mirrors on one side and booths on the other. It was nearly midnight, and the place was full. We pulled our suitcases inside the door and stopped. A blocky guy with short gray hair came toward us, wearing what seemed to be the uniform: short-sleeved white shirt and khakis.

"Well, if it isn't Charlie Magee," he said and shook Magee's hand. "And this is?"

"Don't call me Charlie. This is Annie Carter. Annie, this is Fred."

"Fred." I shook his hand.

"Can we talk somewhere?" Magee asked.

Fred took us to the back booth and stacked our suitcases against the wall. Magee ordered a pizza.

"Native cuisine?" I asked.

"Ex-pat cuisine," Fred answered. "To drink?"

"San Miguel," Magee said.

"Gin for me, with a cube," I said.

The drinks came fast.

"What have you heard about Glenn Rowlandson?" I asked.

"Nothing. Not a damn thing, and the guide hasn't come back either."

"That's not good," I said, as I lifted a piece of pizza, strings of cheese following it up.

"No, it's not," Fred said.

"We're going to have to go after him," I said, pulling the strings of cheese up onto the pizza piece.

Fred looked at Magee. "Is she crazy?"

"Probably, but we have to go after him."

I licked my fingers and wiped them on a paper napkin. "Good pizza. I figure we do the same thing as Rowlandson did. We fly as close as we can get to the river, pick up a guide, drive to the river, and cross it."

"Look, if Rowlandson's been caught, you can't go up the trail."

"Of course not. We go up a parallel trail. Can you get us a guide for tomorrow?"

Fred looked at Magee.

"Well, can you get us a guide for tomorrow?" Magee asked.

"Not for tomorrow. Not this late. The next day. You can do some sightseeing—the palace, the Golden Buddha, you know."

"So do it," I said. "Half when we leave and half when we get back. In gold."

"That'll work. I'll get his brother. He's been worrying."

"Fine. We need guns."

He looked at Magee again.

"She knows what she wants," Magee said.

Fred looked back at me. "What do you want?"

"A Browning 9 mm, spare mag, box of hollow points. Magee?"

"The same."

"How much?" I asked.

"Depends on what you're paying in."

"Dollars?"

"Be the cheapest," he said and led us through a back door to his office. He told me how much, and I laid the dollars down. It didn't look like a dickering kind of place.

Fred ordered coffee for us, and he and Magee sat telling lies to each other about the war. It only took a half an hour for the guns to come. We stripped them down and put them back together again. I nodded and said, "We'll need a hotel for the night."

Fred looked at Magee.

I slapped the desk. "Would you stop doing that! I'm running this show. He's only along because he speaks the lingo."

He looked at Magee.

"She's the boss. I'm only here because I speak the lingo."

Fred got us a hotel room and went outside to put us in a taxi. "I still say you're crazy."

"Don't we know it," Magee said.

Bangkok, the sex capital of the world, had hotel rooms with twin beds? I gave thanks, took off my boots, and fell on my face into one of them.

"Take a shower first," Magee advised.

"Tomorrow."

The day was well advanced when I woke. I heard Magee whistling in the shower. When he came out of the bathroom, I got some clean clothes out and took his place. A long sleep and a long shower might help me make it through the day.

The hotel served breakfast on a terrace overlooking the river. It was humid but not too hot to breathe, so we took a table. Fruit. Lots of fruit, a treat after February in Baltimore. Otherwise, the menu provided breakfast in Western and Eastern varieties. I looked at the noodle offerings and decided not to push my luck. Magee's eyes brightened, and he ordered *phở*. When the noodles came he inhaled happily.

"Haven't had any since Viet Nam."

I ate my unadventurous eggs and bacon and watched the traffic on the river. I finished with another cup of coffee.

"What do we do today?" I asked. "Surely we need some supplies."

"Yeah. We need some Cs and some water tablets."

After breakfast we returned to the Paris Bar. Fred agreed to let us leave our luggage there and had two tickets to Sakon Nakhon airport waiting for us. The guide would have supplies and a Jeep. I paid for the tickets and looked at Magee.

"Let's go back to the room," I said.

"Don't you want to see the Golden Buddha?"

"What I want now is sleep. I'm still working on Baltimore time, and I figure tomorrow is going to be a busy day."

At six thirty the next morning, we boarded a DC-3 for our flight to Sakon Nakhon. The plane looked as if it had escaped from a World War II movie. The name of the airline was written in Thai, and we were the only round eyes on board. Our fellow passengers and the cabin crew looked at us curiously.

"I think they think we're CIA," I said.

"No, the Agency has its own planes."

"And they're much newer than this one," I said.

It'd been a long time since I'd flown on a DC-3, and I'd forgotten its thrusting forward flying attitude. It acted as if it was swimming in heavy surf. Heavy rough surf. The seats had lost their springs sometime around 1945, and the passengers, mostly men, spent the flight chain-smoking. After a couple of hours, we landed at a small airfield with a little bounce and taxied up to the terminal. As we walked down the steps, I saw the passengers for the return trip waiting, one with a crate of chickens and another with a tied-up pig. A short brown man with a round face and black hair parted in the middle and slicked back approached us.

"Mr. Magee?"

"That's me, but she's the boss."

I nodded. "I'm Annie."

He shrugged. "I'm Muong Sui," he said and led the way to a Jeep as old as the airplane was. Since we had not been in Thailand during World War II, I wondered where the equipment had come from. Still, both were well-made and probably in use around the world.

"Ninety miles," he said.

Might as well emphasize the boss part, I thought as I slung my pack into the front passenger side and got in. Magee slung his pack into the back and got in. We drove a little south of east if the sun was any gauge, through dry and harvested rice paddy land, through little villages with rice on tarps beside the road. Women wearing straw hats threw it up and down in baskets to let the wind take the chaff. Children yelled and waved at us. A couple of chickens and two little boys wearing only T-shirts wandered out in front of us. We stopped and a woman retrieved the kids and shooed the chickens to the side of the road. The women waved too, and we waved back. We ditched the Jeep before we got to the river, put on the straw hats the locals were wearing, and walked toward the river. The Mekong was about a half-mile wide at that point, and the water was low because it was the dry season. Small islands and rocks and boulders poked up out of the water. Muong pushed aside a tree limb leaning over the bank and pulled out a small motorized canoe. He put us in front, told us to bend down to hide our height, and started the engine. It made very little noise over the sound of the river. He took us first to a large island. He said something to Magee, and Magee got out and carefully crawled to the top of the island and looked at the other bank. He got back in the boat, shaking his head.

"It's okay," he said.

Muong sailed us around the island and around the boulders to the far shore, where he worked the boat under another tree limb and tied it. I was going to get up, but Magee pushed me back down.

"Let's wait a while," he said.

We waited a while. When nothing hostile came out of the jungle, Magee helped me out of the boat, and we started walking up the trail, Muong leading, me in the middle, and Magee in the rear. While the land on the Thai side of the river was flat and cultivated, on the Lao side, jungle came right down to the river. The trail went steadily up under a triple forest canopy. On either side of the trail stood tall trees with vines linking them in a mat. Underbrush almost as tall as I filled in the space between the trees. As we walked I heard excited bird calls warning the neighborhood of an invasion, and I could see monkeys swinging from limb to limb, chattering their own kind of warning. It was hot and damp and still. And humid. God, it was humid. It smelled of damp and rot. Some of the vines crossed the trail over our heads and crept down, and Muong had to hack them with his machete. The trail went upward at what seemed to me to be a forty-five degree angle, and the surface was damp, made up of last year's rotting leaves. In the distance, I could hear the trickle of water, a small stream going down to the river.

I was wearing a long-sleeved black shirt buttoned up to my chin and long black pants, with the ends tucked into my boots. Taking Magee's advice, I had slathered insect repellent all over anything that showed, a wise decision, because clouds of insects swarmed around my face, and I had trouble keeping them out of my nose. I wondered how soon the sweat pouring down my face would obliterate the insect repellent. If it was hot and sticky when I got off the plane, it was hotter and stickier in the jungle, and not a breath of air seemed to move. I swore never to complain about the heat and humidity in Baltimore in August again.

If only Vivian Rowlandson had gotten somebody else's name out of the Yellow Pages.

We climbed steadily for an hour and then, stepping off the trail into the jungle, stopped to rest.

"Be careful where you put your feet," Magee warned. "There are snakes and scorpions."

He didn't warn me soon enough. I put my foot down and the stick I was standing on raised its head and hissed. I stood frozen. Muong slashed with his machete, and the snake's head fell to the ground. Magee grabbed me. Otherwise, I think I would have fallen.

We squatted and had a little water. By the time my thighs were screaming, Muong motioned us back to the trail, and we started up again. I had the feeling that neither Magee nor Muong would have stopped that soon, but I was red in the face and starting to pant. I was slowing them down. I sighed and reached down inside myself for my big girl panties and put them on. I got us into this. The least I could do was keep up.

It was beginning to get dark, and I was about to drop, when Muong stepped off the trail.

"Can't sleep in the jungle. There is a village nearby."

"How safe is it?" Magee asked.

"Pretty safe. Have a cousin who lives there."

Magee looked at me, and I shrugged my shoulders. "We really can't sleep in the jungle. We'll just have to take a chance."

Muong led us up a side trail, and soon we came to a cluster of houses built on stilts on the side of the hill. The thatched cottages overlooked dry and harvested fields.

"Dry rice," Magee said.

We waited while Muong went to one of the houses. It was a half an hour before he returned.

"My cousin says wait until dark. One of the villagers works for the government."

We squatted at the edge of the clearing until Muong's cousin came for us. He led us to his house, a rectangular board building with a thatched roof and wide open spaces for windows. Flights of stairs went up at each end. The interior was one big room, except for a small area marked off at one end, which served as a kitchen. I could see a woman squatting beside a fire on the floor. The floor was bamboo slats butted against each other. There were two posts holding up the roof, each with a hammock hanging from it. Brightly colored cushions served as furniture. There was nothing else, except for a cupboard on the wall beside the kitchen with a stack of mattresses beside it.

Muong's cousin bowed and shook our hands.

"Cousin have no English," Muong said.

Our host took a jug from the cupboard and poured liquid into some cups, handing each of us one. I sniffed and identified white lightning. I sipped, and tears came to my eyes. It was very strong, good for my aching muscles, but I figured a whole cup of it would put me out.

Muong began to question his cousin, then turned to translate for us.

"The colonel, Phi, and my brother were here two days ago. They rest for a day. The colonel is sick."

I looked at Magee. "Maybe we can catch them tomorrow," I said.

"Maybe," Magee replied.

Three children played quietly in the corner while the adults talked. Soon we were offered stew in a wooden bowl. It was delicious, but I thought it better not to ask what was in it. Soon afterward, our host pulled three mattresses out from the wall and hooked up the hammocks. We and the children slept on mattresses, and I declined to worry about mosquitoes. I was asleep before the light went out.

We were awakened before dawn, given some more stew, and led to the edge of the jungle. We waited until it was light enough to see and went back to the main jungle trail, starting uphill again. We marched until I was red in the face again, and we stopped for water.

"They'll have made it to the next village," Magee said. "How far is that?"

"Maybe two hours," Muong said.

We had been marching for a couple of hours when we heard something coming fast down the trail. We moved silently into the jungle and saw a Hmong man running as if his life depended on it.

Muong hissed. "My brother! Grab him!"

Magee ran forward and grabbed the guy with his arm around the guy's waist and his hand over his mouth. The man struggled and looked frantically left and right. When he saw Muong, he relaxed, and Magee took his hand from man's mouth.

"Muong Pha," Muong said as he pointed to the man. "Muong Sui," he said and pointed to himself. "Pha no English."

We squatted down while Muong Sui questioned his brother. When he was finished our Muong turned to us.

"Bad news. Mr. Rowlandson get to next vill. Army come and shoot Mr. Rowlandson and Phi. Shoot dead. My brother get away."

"How?" I asked.

Muong questioned his brother and turned to me. "They go into house, find bag of gold, dump gold on ground, start fighting. He run."

Remembering how fast he was running, I asked, "Are they following him?"

Muong shook his head. "Not know."

"Now we know the answer. They're both dead. Let's get out of here," I said.

We stepped gingerly back onto the trail and began trotting toward the river. It was easier going down than had been going up. We had gone about half a mile when three men with red stars on their caps slipped silently from a side trail in front of us. Poking us with their rifles, they motioned for us to turn around and go back up the trail.

CHAPTER 20

I took it as a good sign when they didn't shoot us out of hand. I took it as an even better sign that they hadn't noticed I had a gun when they disarmed Magee and the two Hmongs.

The line of march was simple. Magee led off, followed by one of them, followed by me. There was one behind me, then the two Muongs, and one of them bringing up the rear. They moved us along pretty fast, and it wasn't long before I was red in the face and out of breath again. I put my right hand on my side as if it hurt.

"Prepare to move," I said quietly to Magee and went as if to trip. "Oof!" I said, went down, rolled, pulled the pistol, and fired into the face of the man behind me. He landed on top of me, scattering blood and brains on me. I heard a crack as Magee dispatched his guard. I turned to the sound of scuffling behind me and saw the Hmongs taking care of their man. Magee kicked the body off of me and helped me up, and I willed myself to stay upright and turned to vomit on the body. Magee poured water on his handkerchief and cleaned my face and kissed me.

"There's not much I can do about the shirt."

"There's a T-shirt in my pack."

He found it, and I stripped my shirt off, using the back of it to clean my chest. I put the T-shirt on and didn't worry about my bare arms. The mosquitoes would be kept away by the smell. Magee gave me the water bottle and I washed out my mouth, which was a great improvement.

"Magee, we've got to go!"

The radio my man had clipped to his waist began squawking, and Magee grabbed it.

"Who speaks Lao?" he asked.

Muong Sui waved his hand and took the radio.

Magee said, "Tell them it was an accident."

Muong spoke to the radio.

Without consulting each other, we pulled the men off of the trail, and Magee and the Hmongs picked up their rifles. Magee relieved one of them of his pistol, and Muong Sui retrieved his machete. I looked at my gun. I loathed it, but I picked it up and seated in my holster.

"We've got to go," I repeated. "They'll send someone."

We began to jog toward the river. There seemed to be more overhanging vines and tree limbs than there had been going up, and Muong whacked them aside as he ran by. None of them hissed.

Magee looked at me. "You're a good girl," he said.

"Thank you," I replied. I had actually killed a man, and some of his blood and brains were still on me. I shivered. Magee looked at me, and I shook my head. "I'm okay." This was not the time to give in to nerves.

We ran on for about fifteen minutes, and then I had to stop. I bent over and put my hands on my knees. Gradually, my breathing returned to normal. I took a drink of water, and we started running again. I was holding them back. We ran on until we heard a vehicle behind us. I looked at Magee. A bend in the trail was coming up, and I said, "Ambush?"

He nodded.

We ran around the curve. Magee put the Hmongs on the right side of the trail and we crossed to the left, where the driver would be.

"Stand just behind me," he ordered.

I drew my pistol and obeyed. We stood quietly just inside the tree line, waiting. An open vehicle with four soldiers in it came around the bend, and we fired. We were close enough that my 9 mm could do some damage, although I'm not sure I hit anything, but the men's rifles did their deadly work. We dragged the soldiers out of the vehicle into the jungle and took their rifles. That made seven. We got in, with Magee driving, and pelted down the trail.

It was much easier going down the trail with a ride. It was nearly dusk when we reached the river with no more interference. We piled out, taking the three extra rifles with us. The Hmongs had stripped the magazines from the weapons and threw all but one of them as far into the river as they could. The extra they gave to me, although what I could do with it remained to be seen. Magee and the Hmongs shoved the vehicle into the river, where it sank in over its hood. Muong Sui's boat was still safely under the tree. We climbed in, Magee and I bending over to disguise our height again. Muong Sui started the engine and headed for an island, a one-hundred-foot bump of soil near the Thai bank. It had been shaped into a cone by the force of the river current. A small lonely tree stood on the summit, and some new grass sprouted, the result of the dry season.

Before we could get to the island, Lao soldiers reached the bank and started shooting at us. Muong swung us around the island, and we got out. He turned the boat over and shoved it into the current, hoping the soldiers would think they had hit us. We heard the sound of a large engine approaching. Magee crawled up to the summit for a look.

"Muong, come see what this is," he said.

They came back down and consulted. "He thinks it's a Coast Guard boat. We need to get ready."

Magee took my rifle and showed me the selector switch. He put it on full automatic and handed it back to me. "When I give the word, pull the trigger and hold it until you run out of ammunition."

The men lay down on their stomachs, and I followed suit, getting a little ways away from them, in hopes I would shoot only the bad guys. The boat came around the edge of the island, and we began firing. Several of the men on the boat fell overboard, but the boat pulled around the southern edge of the island,

and we stopped firing. I was out of ammunition. I looked toward Magee, and he took my rifle and replaced the magazine. Pity he hadn't taught me to fire a rifle before we left home. We heard the sound of the motor stop, and we knew that the remaining troops had come ashore.

Magee crawled to the top of the island again and looked over. He waved us to follow. There were still four Laotian soldiers, and they were heading toward us.

"Wait for it," Magee said. So we waited. It was not quite dark when we opened fire again. This time we killed them all.

"They're going to miss the boat soon," Magee said. "This island is on the Thai side of the river, but that won't stop them. We have to get across to the Thai bank and get as far away from it as we can as soon as possible."

He walked into the river using his rifle as a walking stick to see how deep the water was. Right there, the water came up to his knees. He came back and lined us up, Magee, then me, then the two Hmongs, who were sturdy but shorter than I. We started into the river, the current pushing our legs hard. The water got a little deeper, but not much. We walked around some smooth rocks. We were halfway across when I stepped into a hole and went under. Magee jerked me up, as I sputtered and spit water. I shook my head and let go of Magee's hand. The Browning was still seated in its holster, but it was soaked, along with my pack and rifle.

We walked around more boulders, going more carefully this time. We made it across, climbed up the bank, and lay down to catch our breath. The men were soaked to their waist or a little above, but I was soaked completely. I thought it would be nice to rest for a while, but Magee said, "We've got to get away from the bank."

"We're in Thailand," I protested.

"They'll still come after us."

I got up wearily and followed the men along a path between stubbled rice paddies. We had walked for about a mile when we heard an engine and dogs barking off to the left. A village. We swung farther to the right, but more dogs barked. We heard yelling, and a shot rang out. The Laotians had followed us. Magee motioned us down, and we squatted in the forward corner of a rice paddy. The yelling went on, and another shot was fired. We'd brought the Laotian Army on an innocent Thai village. I could see men fanning out from the village heading our way. Magee shoved my face down into the stubble, and we waited. The next sounds came from engines behind us. Despite Magee, I looked up and saw a new, and larger, group of uniformed men enveloping the first group, pushing them back, back, away from the village and us. Soon we couldn't see them, but we heard their engine fire. The sound moved away, and we heard one more rifle shot. From the Thais saying "and don't come back?"

"Come on," whispered Magee. "They're going to look for us."

There was a small copse of trees about a hundred yards ahead, and we took cover in it. Magee was right. The Thai troops came back and searched the paddies looking for us, but they didn't come as far as the trees.

"You know, after all this, I'm going to need a powerful lot of hugging and kissing when we get back to Bangkok," I said.

It was too dark to see Magee, but I heard him smile. "I can do that," he said.

We settled down in a bunch to sleep. It wasn't really cold, but we were all wet. I woke in the night with Magee's arm around me. I moved, and he tightened it. "Starting early," he whispered.

I woke at dawn, stiff and sore and still damp. I fetched out some Cs and handed them around. My roll of *baht* had been in the waterproof zip compartment in the pack, so it was dry. I gave the money to Magee, who was drier than I, and he stuffed it in his shirt pocket. Behind the dawn birdsong, I could hear sounds of traffic.

"There's a road over there," I said and pointed. After we finished eating and burying the tin cans, we ditched the rifles and Muong's machete. I put my gun and holster in my pack, because my T-shirt wouldn't cover them, and we walked to the sound of the traffic. We needed to know where we were and how to get back to Bangkok. It wasn't long before a gaily painted bus stopped for us. Muong Sui asked the driver a question and turned to me. "Four hours to Sakon Nakhon. We go?"

Magee was the guy with the money. I poked him, and he said, "We go." He peeled off some bills and gave them to the driver, and we boarded the bus.

It was just as gay inside as it had been outside. Multicolored bobble fringe decorated the windshield and all down both sides of the windows. A Buddha statue stood on the dashboard, and number of amulets hung from the rearview mirror, which was good, considering the way the guy drove. The passengers stared at us as we walked back and took our seats in the back row. There were no springs in the seat and seemingly hadn't been for years. The driver closed the door and turned up the radio. I took out my water bottle and took a heavy drink. Four hours with no springs and Thai pop music. Was it worse than what Thai soldiers could have done to us? I was so tired that I put my head on Magee's shoulder and tried to sleep, but it seemed as though the driver stopped every five feet to take somebody on or let somebody off. I was so exhausted I finally fell asleep. When he woke me I was sticky, my clothes were more or less dry, and we were in Sakon Nakhon. We had something to eat and took a taxi to the airport, where Magee bought four tickets to Bangkok. The daily flight would depart in two hours, so we took seats in molded orange plastic chairs in the terminal and waited.

The plane came in from Bangkok, and we walked across the flight line to find the same woman with a crate of chickens and man with a trussed-up pig waiting to board the plane. Maybe it was a tradition? I was eager to see what the guy was going to do with the pig. After the passengers from Bangkok got off, we climbed up the stairs into the plane. We took our seats, and I waited. After everybody else had gotten on, the man with the pig came down the aisle, holding it by a strap as if it were a suitcase. He took the seat across the aisle from me and shoved the pig under the seat in front.

The pig squealed in protest.

CHAPTER 21

Bangkok

"We've got to find some place to stash these guys until I can get them to swear that Glenn Rowlandson is dead," I said to Magee as we got off the plane in Bangkok.

"The CIA's got a safe house over the Paris Bar."

"Sounds good, if they will let us use it. Is there a back way into the bar?"

"Yeah. I'll call Fred and tell him to expect us."

I've been in some noisome alleys in my time, but the one leading to the Paris Bar was the worst I've ever smelled. Maybe it was the heat and humidity, or maybe the things rotting in it didn't exist in Baltimore. Magee knocked on the door, and Fred let us in. Fred called the CIA station chief and handed me the phone.

"The guy's name is Tony Baker."

"Mr. Baker, my name's Anne Carter. I'm a Baltimore PI. I've been looking for Glenn Rowlandson."

There was a stunned silence. Then he asked, "Did you find him?"

"Yes, I did, and that's the reason I'm calling. He hired a guide Fred recommended, and the guide tells us the Laotian army caught and executed Rowlandson and Phi. Their guide is our guide's brother. I need to stash them somewhere until I can get them to the embassy tomorrow to swear to their story. I hear you have a safe house over the Paris Bar."

"Where did you hear that?"

"General knowledge. I think they're probably your people anyway, since they go up into Laos regularly. You may not want to use them for a while. It got a little hairy when we were coming out. Can I use your safe house?"

"Rowlandson's dead?"

"I just said so. I've got to get Muong Pha to tell his story and swear to it."

"I need the story."

"Look, all I need is the key."

"And I've got the key. I'll be there in ten minutes."

While we were waiting, the boys had beers, and I had gin, and we all had pizza. Baker appeared at the back door looking secretive, although I presume every taxi driver in town knew his name and probably his home address. He was a stocky guy with a bunch of white hair wearing a short-sleeved white shirt and khaki pants. He sat down and had a beer and a piece of the pizza.

"Tell me," he said through a mouthful of cheese. "You went in?" He sounded amazed.

"We did," I responded.

"Why? You could have got the same thing Rowlandson did, a bullet in the head."

"A matter of an inheritance. We came to get him to sign a document turning over his property to his wife."

"Why?"

"Because he was dying of pancreatic cancer, and he left her without much money. If he didn't turn the property over to her and he died in Laos, it would take her years to have him declared legally dead. Did you know him?"

"I did. He was a strange duck. They couldn't keep him out of the field."

"He was going up there to die. I think he had a woman, possibly a family, there. But he had a wife in Baltimore and a twenty-five-acre estate. He left her little money to run it. There were other reasons, but that's basically it. Do you have Hmong?" I asked.

He shook his head no, so I told him the story.

"And you knew what it's like to get into Laos?"

"We knew," I said.

"It got hairy? Hairy how?"

I began to tell that tale. By the time we took down the first three Laotians, Fred and the station chief were looking incredulous.

I began to get angry. "Look, this will go faster if you stop making little cries of incredulity."

"You did what?" the chief repeated.

"I was the only one armed. I fell down and rolled over and shot my guard. Magee and the Muongs took care of theirs. We rolled them into the jungle and started running."

Magee took up the story, and they got more incredulous.

I got angrier. "Who do you think I am? Shirley Temple?"

Magee looked at me and grinned. "Well, I didn't know either."

"Yeah, but you didn't stare at me like I'm some kind of damned freak," I fumed.

Magee ignored that. "How many do you think we took out, altogether?" he asked.

I began to count. "Three on the trail, four in the ambush, four in the boat, three on the island. That's eleven."

"It was getting dark, and I couldn't see very well, but I figure altogether maybe twenty."

"Twenty-three," said Muong Sui.

The station chief just looked at me.

I glared at him.

"I figure she's a natural," Magee said. "Now, can we use your safe house?"

He handed me the key and went off shaking his head.

I gave the key to Magee. "You guys go ahead. I've got to talk to the legal attaché at the embassy."

I used Fred's phone again. The attaché's name was John Chalmers.

"I've got to get a story from a Hmong man recorded, interpreted, and attested to. It's a matter of

216

inheritance," I told him. "Do you have a Hmong interpreter?"

"I've got a Hmong interpreter but no way to type the Hmong text. If it's a matter for court testimony, we will have to record the Hmong testimony on tape, attest to that, and give you the tape to take with you."

"I hope they have a Hmong interpreter in Baltimore," I said. "What time?"

We settled on ten o'clock the next morning.

"I'm going upstairs now," I told Fred. "Can you send some dinner up?"

"Sure," he replied. "What do you want?"

"I don't care. Anything that you think the Hmongs will eat. And beer."

"Hamburgers and fries be okay? I know they'll eat that."

"That's fine. And gin."

I went upstairs to the apartment, a living room, kitchen, two bedrooms, and bath. The guys were sitting on the sofa. Magee flipped the TV channels until he found a soccer match for them.

"Dinner is coming. Hamburgers and French fries okay?"

Two of them nodded, and Magee told the third, who nodded.

"Our suitcases are here, but we've got to get them some clean clothes," I told Magee.

He collected sizes from the men and went down to talk to Fred. By the time we had finished eating, Fred had come up with the clothes.

"I'm taking one of the bedrooms. They can have the other. I'm afraid you get the sofa. I don't think they'll try to leave, but . . ."

"Yeah."

"I didn't intend to spend this night alone."

"Me neither," Magee said. I must've looked woebegone, because he put his arms around me and whispered, "It's only another half day."

"I don't think I can go on being blasé for much longer," I whispered back.

The US Embassy in Bangkok was a monstrous five-story building, as long as two city blocks. This was not because of all the business we had to do with the Royal Kingdom of Thailand but because the secret war in Laos had been directed from the building. Now that the war was over, they could go a long way to erasing the national debt by dividing it into apartments and renting them out.

The legal attaché, John Chalmers, was the first person working for the State Department that I ever met who looked like a diplomat. It was probably the blue blazer. He was a tall man with short brown hair and an aristocratic face. Beside his desk stood the interpreter, a slender Asian woman with long black hair and an ivory complexion. After everyone had been introduced, he led us to a conference room and seated us at a round table. He took orders for coffee and tea, put a tape recorder in the middle of the table, and got right down to it.

"Would you explain the situation to me, Miss Carter?" he said.

"Colonel Glenn Rowlandson, a retired Special Forces officer, disappeared from his home outside Baltimore several weeks ago. His wife hired me to find him. My investigation revealed that he was dying of pancreatic cancer and that he had come to Thailand to try to get to a village in Laos where he had been during the Vietnamese war. The colonel left his wife with very little money. Her father had left his entire estate to Rowlandson rather than his daughter."

"Surely that's unusual," Chalmers said.

"It was. It's a long story that you don't need. It became necessary to take a document turning over the property to Mrs. Rowlandson to him for his signature, because if Rowlandson died in Laos, Mrs. Rowlandson would have to wait a long time to have him declared legally dead." I leaned back in my chair and hoped this would be the last time I had to tell that story. "Mr. Magee and I came to Bangkok to follow his trail to get his signature. Mr. Muong Pha"—I pointed to him—"was Rowlandson's guide. It's his story we need attested to."

The coffees and teas came and we sugared and creamed, and Muong Pha began his story, talking into the tape recorder. The translator spoke into another tape recorder. When they were finished, Mr. Baker said, "We'll have to have the English version typed. Would you like to come back tomorrow and sign it?"

Magee and I exchanged glances. "Can you type it up right now? If there's a place where we can get a sandwich nearby, we can do it all today. These gentlemen would like to get home, and so would we."

Baker frowned. I was interfering with his office's schedule, but after a little bit of convincing, he agreed and told us where the lunchroom was. We returned to his office in two hours, and we began reading and signing. Magee and Muong Sui signed the English version. I signed a codicil stating that the English translation represented the translation of what Muong Pha had told me, and Muong Pha made his mark on the English version. Baker put the tape into the recorder, and Magee and Muong Sui attested to the Hmong version. I got three copies of the English version and hoped one copy of the tape would be adequate.

We left the embassy and walked to a café, where I joined the men in having a beer.

I looked around the table. "I never want to tell that story again!" I said to the world in general.

We held up our beers and clicked cans. We drank our beers quietly, saying nothing. We had said all we had to say to each other. When we finished I reached into the watch pocket of my jeans and took out two gold bars. I gave one to each man, and we shook hands. They went off to look for the bus station, and Magee and I went back to the hotel.

The first thing I did was call Elizabeth, and I got a shock.

"Mama, we're getting married! When are you coming home?"

"Married!"

I turned to Magee. "They're getting married! Since when?" I asked Elizabeth.

"Since yesterday. I decided that the only way to stop him from proposing to me was to marry him."

Jack came online. "Annie, we're really going to do it. We're going to have a big white wedding!"

I heard wrestling for the phone. "No we're not. We're eloping to Elkton."

The chief business of Elkton, Maryland, was runaway marriages.

Jack snatched the phone back. "I've waited for so long that I think I deserve a big wedding."

"Take what you can get, Jack," I said. "Elizabeth won't stand for a big wedding, and I won't pay for one. You get it planned. We'll be home in four days. Let me speak to Elizabeth.

"We'll be home in four days, and you can get married," I told her.

"You will wear a dress, Mama, won't you?"

"I will wear a dress, and Magee will wear a tie, even if he has to buy one."

I sat down on the bed. "Well! We should go out of town more often."

"What do you mean I'll wear a tie?"

"You'll wear a tie. I hope this will be a once-in-a-lifetime event."

"I wore ties to my weddings. I think I jinxed them."

"Third time's a charm. Besides it's not you who's getting married."

It was still office hours in Baltimore. I put in a call to Archibald Withers, Glenn Rowlandson's attorney. "Mr. Withers, I found Glenn Rowlandson."

"Where?" he asked.

"In Laos, and he's dead. I'm faxing you the story. It's a long one and I don't want to tell it over the phone. I'll be home in two or three days, and I'll come to see you after you've read it. I also have a tape recording for you. It contains the original Hmong testimony."

"Hmong?"

"Yes. When you get the document, it will all become clear."

He wanted to go on asking questions, but I hung up.

I took a sheet of hotel stationery and wrote a cover page for the fax, took it down to the business center, and faxed it to Withers.

Back in the room I said, "Now all we have to do is go home."

"Not quite," Magee said, and put his arms around me.

I leaned close. "Could I stop being brave now?" I started crying.

He held me tight and said, "Yes, you can stop being brave. You can cry as much as you like. After that, it's my turn."

We stayed in bed for the best part of two days, resting and making love. We did get up for the occasional meal. Before we left, we went back to the Paris Bar to see Fred and have a pizza.

I handed him the Browning. "I'd like to sell you a gently used pistol. Only killed one man," I said. "Three quarters of what I paid for it."

"Yeah, but you fired it a second time," Magee said.

"I know, but I don't think I hit anything."

I ended up settling for half.

CHAPTER 22

Baltimore

I looked out the window as we flew into the sun. Why had I done that—endangering both of our lives by going into Laos? Okay, I felt sorry for Vivian Rowlandson, but sorry enough to get us shot? There's always been something perverse about me. In high school, the girls took home ec and the boys took mechanical drawing. I took mechanical drawing. I wasn't very good at it, but I took it and passed. I learned to cook later but not very well. When I told my father I was going to marry Milton, he tried to talk me out of it. He said I wouldn't like it. I married Milton and found that father had been right. I didn't like it. Instead of getting a job as a secretary or clerk in a department store, I had to become a detective. It wasn't really that I made more money as detective, although I did. It was just that I didn't want to be a secretary. I don't do girl things easily or well. I turned to Magee.

"Why did I do that?"

"Do what?"

"Risk our lives in Laos."

"You said you felt sorry for Vivian Rowlandson."

"I know that's what I said, but was that really the reason?"

He looked down the aisle at the stewardesses preparing to serve drinks. "I think you just wanted to prove you could do it."

"And you went with me and risked your life?"

He said, with that black Irish grin, "I wanted to see if you could do it too."

"You let me risk your life?"

"Listen, I didn't *let* you risk my life. *I* risked my life because I chose to," he said. This time he gave me a black Irish frown.

The plane got in close to midnight, and by the time we got home, I felt as if a tank had run over me.

"Hugging and kissing?" Magee asked.

"Now that's an idea," I said.

CHAPTER 23

Archibald Withers had the document on his desk when we went into his office. He looked distressed. "Do you believe this person?"

I looked at Magee.

"Yes, I do," Magee said. "Muong Pha was out in the jungle for several days before he could get loose to run for the river. They almost killed us. It goes without saying that if they find a round eye in one of the vills they'll kill him."

"Then why did he go? If he knew they'd kill him, why did he go?" Withers asked.

"He was dying, Mr. Withers. He wanted to die there," I said. "I believe he had a woman there, possibly a family. It's the village he kept going back to during the war."

I reached into my pack and pulled out the tape. "This is a copy of the Hmong testimony. You may need it for the court. Where you'll find a Hmong translator, I have no idea, but it's here to testify to the veracity of the English translation." I handed it to him. "Are these documents enough for you to begin probate?"

"It's going to be a complex problem," he said. "I need to talk to Mrs. Rowlandson."

"I'm going out to see her now. She doesn't know he's dead yet. I didn't think it was the sort of thing I ought to tell her over the telephone. Would you like to talk with her later in the day?"

"I think it would be better if I called her," he said. "I'll call her this afternoon. Do you have a number?"

I gave him her number; we shook hands and left.

Driving out Reisterstown Road, I noticed all but a few small patches of snow had melted. As we drove up the lane to The Gables, I saw the horses out in the pasture. She must have hired a stable boy. I rang the bell. She looked surprised to see us.

"It's not good news," she said immediately.

"No, it's not," I replied.

She led us to her sitting room and went over to the mantel and pulled the cord to call Phi before she remembered he wasn't there. She looked confused.

"We don't need any tea, Vivian." I handed her a copy of Muong's testimony, and she sat down with it in her hand, afraid to look at it. "Read it, Vivian. After you do, you need to talk to Mr. Withers."

Her hand was shaking so badly that she couldn't read the text. She put it in her lap and began to read. As she read, she began to cry. When she finished she threw it on the coffee table and covered her face.

Great wracking sobs shook her body. I went and sat beside her and put my arms around her and gradually the sobs subsided.

"There was a woman there," she said.

"We believe so," I said.

"He never loved me, you know," she said in a distant voice. "I don't know why he married me. Daddy's money, perhaps. But we were all right until he went to the war. When he came back, he had changed. I thought it was because he was sick. At least I told myself it was because he was sick, but I think I knew all along that he had a woman there. He kept going back." She looked out the window to the pasture. "What will I do now?" she asked in a mournful voice.

"You're going to sell the horses, put this place on the market, and get out of here. This place ate your mother, and it's eating you. You need to go somewhere where it's warm, find a decrepit charter boat captain, and start melting the ice around your heart. You're a young woman, Vivian. You deserve love."

She looked astonished.

"I mean it, you deserve to be loved and to love. The probate of his will may take a long time. It's going to be incredibly complicated, because the testimony to your husband's death comes from a Hmong man, translated into English. As soon as Mr. Withers is named executor of your husband's estate, he can put this place on the market. In the meantime, you need to leave. There's not a single happy memory for you in this place."

"Where should I go?"

"Anywhere you want to. The islands? The south of France? Anywhere."

As we left I could see that the idea was beginning to take hold. There were questions in her eyes, but they weren't the same questions she'd had when she hired me.

I had a big white wedding when I married Milton, but planning it was nothing like planning Elizabeth and Jack's elopement. I called and made reservations at the chapel. They asked me what kind of music and flowers I wanted. That was it.

Elizabeth had to have a dress. I had to have a dress. Jack had to have a suit. Magee rebelled at having a suit, settling for a new jacket and a tie. The one he had was black and suitable only for funerals.

Elizabeth didn't have a big white dress, only a little sky blue dress that matched her eyes. There weren't hundreds of people there. Only me and Magee.

On the appointed day we drove up I-95 in two cars—the boys in Magee's Jeep and the girls in Jack's car. The wedding chapel was an old stone building dating, perhaps, to the revolution. The woodwork suggested that it did. The little chapel and the flowers on the altar looked lovely. Elizabeth's bouquet was composed of white lilies with a few colored snapdragons and baby's breath. Jack insisted on the snapdragons. I guess she had snapped enough at him. The organist diddled a little classical music while we got ourselves in position—the guys in front waiting for the bride, with me leading her down the aisle to witness her marriage and give her away at the same time. It was a generic wedding service, composed of several religious ceremonies, leaning heavily on the Episcopalian. Magee disappeared after handing Jack the ring, and we processed out into the lobby to the familiar "here comes the bride" music. Magee came back, grinning. Elizabeth threw her bouquet at me, and I caught it under protest. We stepped outside and found Jack's car had been decorated by Magee—"just married" in soap and streamers and tin cans tied to the bumper. They drove away waving. When we finished waving, I threw the bouquet in a trash can, and we walked toward the Jeep.

"You have legs," Magee said. "I never noticed."

"Yes, I do. And high-heeled shoes. I need to sit down before I die."

Magee opened the door for me. "How's your hugging and kissing level?" he asked me.

"Seriously depleted. Weddings are hard work. You?"

"Me too. Let's go home and do something about it."

THE END

ABOUT THE AUTHOR

Marilynn Larew is a retired historian who taught for many years in the University System of Maryland. Besides American history, she taught the history of the Vietnamese war and the history of terrorism, topics she uses in her writing. She likes to set her plots in places she's been or places she'd like to go. She's lived in Baltimore. She just had to dream about Morocco and Dubai. She lives in a southern Pennsylvania in a 200-year-old brick farmhouse with her husband Karl, who is also a historian and author. She has also written the Lee Carruthers series, which includes *The Spider Catchers* and *Dead in Dubai*.

She belongs to the Sisters in Crime, the Guppies, and the Chinese Military History Society.

If you liked this book, please leave a review on Amazon and Goodreads. Reviews mean a lot to an author. They tell her that she's connecting with readers and giving them pleasure.

If you would like news about upcoming events, subscribe to my newsletter at
http://marilynnlarew.com/newsletter/
and receive a free Lee Carruthers short story.